LUCY'S GROOM

HEIDI HARRIS

Scripture

"Enjoy life with your wife, whom you love,

all the days of this meaningless life that God has

given you under the sun all your meaningless

days.

For this is your lot in life and in your toilsome labor

under the sun."

(Ecclesiastes 9:9) NIV

Lucy

One
1

"Are you sure you want to do this?" The postmaster looked at the note again.

"I'm sure." I turned on my heels and let the door close behind me.

"I can't believe you just did that." My sister hissed.

I untied my horse. "Pa can't work no more. What did you expect?" I put my foot in the stirrup. I pushed up and swung my boot to the other side of the horse and slid my boot into the other stirrup.

My kid sister was right behind me. "It's not his fault that he tripped over Patches. She was just trying to get love."

"If Patches wasn't such a good mouser, I would kick her out now." I spit on the ground; the cat made me so mad.

"Patches is a good kitty." My sister muttered.

I shook my head. Sometimes my sister could be so sentimental. I loved her, but we had a farm to run. Sometimes she needed to be practical.

"Now we are a man short. Doc says Pa ain't ever going to walk right after this." I flicked the reins.

"Doc might be wrong. He's been wrong before. He said he could save Ma, and he didn't." Beth Ann raised her voice so I could hear her over the horses.

I've been avoiding marriage for quite some time. I didn't need a man with Pa around. Ever since Ma died, my sister and Pa needed me to help with the farm and help raise Beth Ann.

I glanced at my sister. She was almost raised, and we couldn't run this farm with Pa down. We had just finished harvest season, or we would be in more trouble than we were already in. We were prepared for winter, but right after winter was spring.

Planting season is coming up faster than I wanted to admit. If Doc was right and Pa's leg didn't set right, he wouldn't be able to help me come spring. Doc had pretty much said Pa's hard working days were over. We needed someone to pull Pa's weight around the farm quick.

We didn't have a lot of money, so hiring someone was out of the question. Sending for a mail order husband seemed like the only choice I had. Most of the men around here were already married or not worth marrying.

Home came into view. I couldn't imagine leaving this place. This farm ran through my blood. It was part of me and I was part of it. Beth Ann and I put the horses away once we got back home.

"Beth Ann, can you help me with the storage building?" I pointed to the building closest to the house.

"What for?" Beth Ann scowled.

"If someone replies to my advertisement, I need somewhere to put him. We need all of the stuff in there put in the barn." I wasn't looking forward to the job either, but it needed done.

"Do I have to?" Beth Ann complained.

"Yeah, you have to. It will only take us an hour or two to clean out." I marched over to the building.

It wasn't much to look at, but it would do for now. I opened the door. Beth Ann and I peeked in.

"It might take more than two hours." Beth Ann scowled.

"How about two hours today and two hours tomorrow?" I didn't want to do it by myself.

"Okay, Lucy." Beth Ann stood straighter. "I'll go get some rags and I'll be right back."

"That sounds good." I took off my cowboy hat and put it on the hook right inside of the door. It would be easier to clean out the place without it on.

Beth Ann came running back. "Do you think this is enough rags?" She had a whole basket full.

"I hope so." I smiled at my sister and she giggled.

Luke

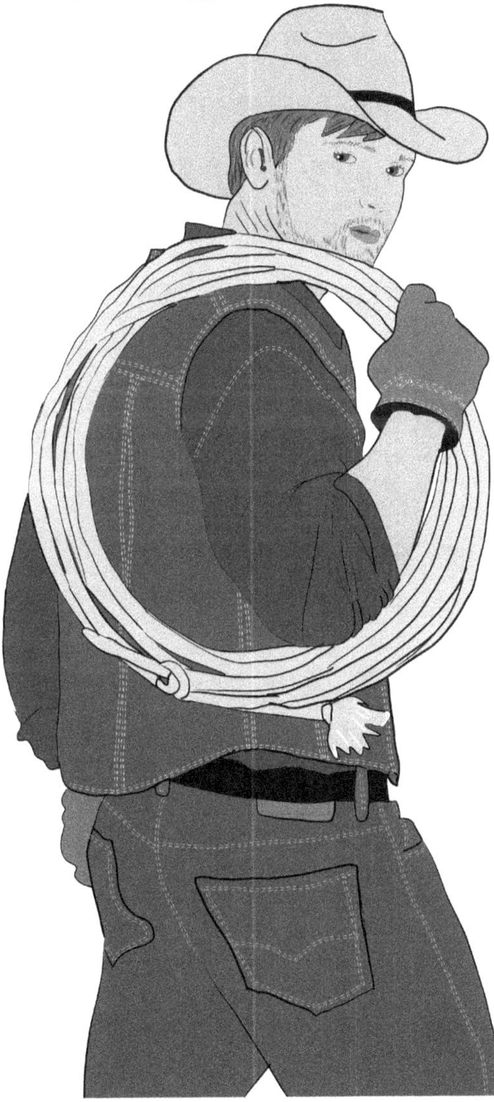

Two

2

I walked to the board for the tenth time this week. I had been looking everywhere for work, but there was none to be had. My uncle was letting us stay out back in the summer kitchen, but it didn't feel right. A man should be able to hold his own.

I frowned. The board was the same as it had been the day before. The postmaster walked over and pinned an advertisement to the board.

"There's an interesting one for you Luke." The postmaster laughed like he had told a good joke.

I stepped closer to read the advertisement. I thought it was a job opportunity. It was more than what I was expecting.

GROOM WANTED

Works Hard

Durable

Man of God

Willing to Relocate

I read it three times. Willing to relocate. I let out a deep breath. I didn't have any other options.

Relocating wasn't ideal, but it would mean I had a real home. If she didn't want to relocate, land was probably involved. I would be able to earn my keep. I wasn't opposed to hard work.

If I had a way to support myself, I had to take it. I wasn't sure what kind of woman would be willing to send for a man, but I couldn't keep living off of my uncle. Uncle Billy let us move into the outside kitchen when we lost the farm, but it didn't sit right with me. Winter was coming. I needed a home of my own.

I pulled a few coins out of my pocket. It was hard to part with the money, but I had to answer before someone else did. This probably wasn't the only town she sent the advertisement to.

"I would like to post a response." I looked the postmaster in the eye.

"Are you sure you don't want to discuss this with your mother or uncle first?" The postmaster was concerned.

"No, sir. I'm a man. I can make my own decisions." I wrote down my response on the back of the advertisement and pushed it to the postmaster.

"Your Pa would have a lot to say if he knew you were responding to this." The postmaster held up the paper.

"If my Pa were still alive, we wouldn't have lost the farm." I grumbled.

The postmaster nodded and started typing on his machine. "It's been sent."

He pushed the paper back towards me. I took it and stuck it in my pocket. Ma would want to read it.

"Thank you." I nodded and left the building.

Now, I had to go break the news to Ma. I didn't see any other choice. Pa hadn't been the best at finances. When he died, the farm was already on the verge of going under.

By the time Ma sold the farm, it was barely enough to pay the bank back and the bills that had mounted since Pa died. Pa was a proud man. I wish I knew we were in trouble before he died. I could have tried to do something, but by the time I knew what was going on, it was too late.

I took my hat off my head and wiped my brow. I let out a deep breath.

"Ma, we got to talk." I let the door fall close behind me.

"Was there work?" Ma put two mugs on the table.

I hung up my hat. I ran my fingers through my hair before sitting down.

"I might have a solution." I put my hands around the mug to warm them. We didn't have enough sup-plies to make it through the winter.

"Solution?" My Mom was concerned.

I pushed the notice towards her. Ma took the paper and picked it up. Her mouth went into a straight line. Finally, she put the paper down.

"No, Luke." Ma shook her head no.

"The decision has already been made." My tone sounded dull to my own ears.

"Luke, you don't have to do this." Ma was upset. "You should marry for love, not to take care of me and Tommy."

"Ma, I've been taking care of this family since Pa died last fall. We ain't gone hungry yet." I swallowed.

It was true, but we've sold everything we could. There wasn't anything left to sell. We barely had enough space in the yard for a small garden for the three of us. Uncle Billy had shared what he could, but he still had a family to feed.

When we moved in with Uncle Billy, we brought our chickens from the farm. The chickens' eggs were keeping something in our bellies. Man can't live on eggs alone. We were gonna have to raid the coffee jar next month if something didn't change.

Lucy

Three
3

Beth Ann had talked me into coming back into town, even though I sent out the ad yesterday. Leaving my farm two days in a row was a waste of my time. I had a fence that needed mended. The sooner I got home, the sooner I could finish my chores.

"Do you think anyone responded, Lucy?" My sister tied up her horse.

I glared at my sister. Part of me wanted to get this over with and the other part of me hoped no one responded. I should have waited until next week to come back.

"Well?" She persisted.

"Be quiet." I hissed.

"Why?" Beth Ann walked with me toward the postmaster.

My sister didn't catch on to subtlety. I wish she could take a hint. I didn't want this town jabbering more than necessary. The only people that knew I put the ad out were Pa, Beth Ann, and the postmaster.

"There's…" My sister ran off to her friend without finishing her sentence.

"Miss Dawson." The postmaster greeted me. "You have a few responses about your ad."

The postmaster turned around. He walked to a box and pulled out some papers. He pushed six pieces of paper across the counter.

I didn't think I'd even get one response to the ad this soon, and I had six? That was surprising. I picked up the one on top and started reading.

How much property do you have?

I snorted. I wasn't a dowry to be given away. I crumbled it up and threw it in the trash can.

I went to the next one.

I don't have the fare. Do you think you could send cash my way?

My mouth fell open when I saw the absurd amount he was asking for. I could build a small homestead for that price.

I'm not willing to relocate, but you're welcome to come here. I have 8 little ones to raise. They need a Ma.

A Ma? Or a workhorse? I shook my head and trashed it too.

How God fearing do you mean? I would be happy to relocate if the price was right.

I crushed it.

The fifth one was too indecent to finish reading. I dropped it into the trash can.

I flipped over the sixth one, praying for a miracle.

Yes to all. Age 19. Luke Larson. I'd have to bring my Ma & bro Tommy w/me.

19. I let out a deep breath. He ought to be young enough to work. I was 22 though. I wasn't sure about the age difference. Young men could be difficult and hardheaded, so could older men, for that matter. It didn't look like I had much choice.

Luke Larson. I stared at the name on the paper. He had a brother and a Ma. That was three more mouths to feed. I calculated the food in the cellar. It should be enough to get six of us through the winter. We might need a bigger garden in the spring.

I tapped the counter. If I married Luke, my name would be Lucy Larson. It was as good of a name as any.

"I'd like to respond to this one." I pushed the remaining paper across the counter.

"Okay." The postmaster eyed me curiously. "Put your response on here." He pushed me a fresh piece of paper with a pencil.

I took the pencil and started writing. I read my response for the third time. I swallowed. This was the most important decision of my life.

"Please send this." I pushed the paper back.

"Are you sure?" The postmaster examined me.

"Yes, sir." I nodded.

The postmaster tapped on his machine.

"It's been sent Miss Dawson. I hope you know what you're doing." The postmaster scowled.

"Me too." I muttered as I left the building.

Luke

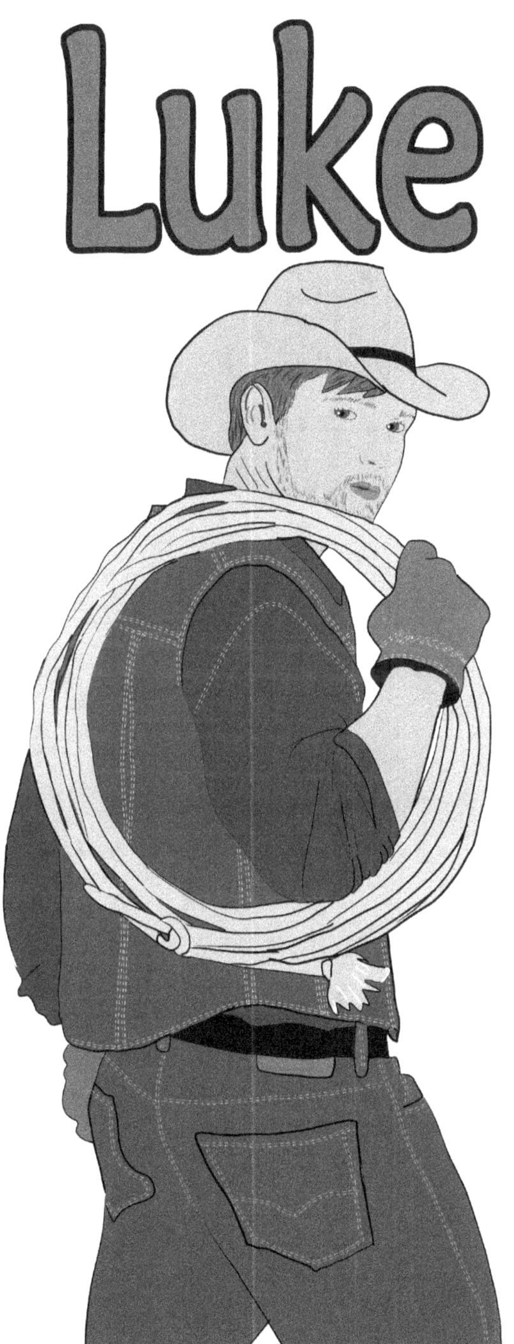

Four
4

The post was closing in thirty minutes. I wanted to give the woman a chance to respond today. I knew it was doubtful that she made the trip into town two days in a row, but it was all I could do to wait for a response.

I put my hat on. My heart was pounding. Would she have responded? What if she says no?

I thought of Ma and Tommy. How was I going to provide for them if she said no? I could always go out west and send money home. Sometimes the mail got lost or was stolen. I'd prefer to take them with me if I left the town I was born in.

I opened the door. The bell rang. I was more nervous than I had been in my life.

"Is there anything for me today?" I took off my hat and ran a hand through my hair before putting it back on.

"Luke, you got a response from yesterday." The postmaster waved a flimsy piece of paper.

"What did she say?" I took it from his hand and walked to the other side of the room.

The postmaster was too busy laughing to answer.

Mr. Larson, come at your earliest convenience. I live with my Pa & sis. Lucy. 22.

An address was listed at the bottom of the page.

Lucy. I looked up at the postmaster.

"Are you really going to go, son?" The postmaster had a teasing smile on his lips.

"I am." I nodded. "I'll be right back." I opened the door.

"I close in twenty minutes." The postmaster called to me as I shut the door.

I ran over to the train station. They were still open. I put the paper on the counter, out of breath.

"Mr. Larson, what is the rush?" Mr. Mathias frowned.

"When does the next train leave for this town?" I pointed at the address.

"Let me see." Mr. Mathias adjusted his glasses.

It felt like an eternity as he slowly picked up a paper next to him. My heart thumped in my chest. My mind was racing. I knew my life was about to change forever.

"Tomorrow morning at 9AM and Monday morning at 9AM." Mr. Mathias pointed to his schedule.

Tomorrow wasn't enough time for Lucy to know I was coming. Monday would be a better option. I need to tell Ma, get packed, and say goodbye to our friends and our kin.

"How much does it cost for three tickets?" I leaned on the counter.

Mr. Mathias rattled off a number. I was sure we had that amount left in the coffee can. I didn't like digging into the coffee can any more than Ma did, but we had to get there in order to have a place to live.

"Can I purchase the tickets on Monday?" I was already in the middle of making plans.

"Yes, Mr. Larson. Why do you want to go out there?" Mr. Mathias scowled.

"I have kin out there." I grinned as I tapped the counter twice. I took a step back, away from the counter. "I'll see you Monday, Mr. Mathias."

I rushed back to the postmaster. I took a paper off the counter and jotted down that I would be coming Monday.

"Please send this." I pushed the paper toward the postmaster. I put money on the counter.

The postmaster read the note. "Are you sure?"

I nodded my head.

The postmaster typed on his machine. "It's been sent."

"Thank you." I tipped my hat as I left the building.

It was time to tell Ma and Tommy the news. I really hope they take it well. I let out a deep breath.

Please, Lucy, check your mail tomorrow. I prayed as I made my way home.

Lucy

Five
5

Luke was coming on the train today. By the end of the day, I would be a married woman. I didn't like it, but I didn't see any other options. I needed help with the farm.

I finished milking the cows. I glanced towards the house. Smoke was coming out of the chimney. Our life on the farm was about to change. Three new people were walking into our lives.

I picked up the pail of milk and started walking towards the main house. I walked past the building Luke and I were going to share. It wasn't too big, but it should do for now. Beth Ann and Pa were going to stay in the main house. Tommy and Luke's Ma were going to stay in the outside kitchen. It had a chimney, so they would be warm in the winter.

I put the milk down on the kitchen counter. "Where's Pa?"

"I'm coming." Pa was hobbling towards us. "It's a big day today." He was using two sticks to brace himself.

"Pa, you don't have to come all the way to town." I helped Pa sit at the table.

"I'm coming Lucy." My father's tone was firm.

"Breakfast is ready." Beth Ann put a plate on the table.

"Thanks, Beth Ann." Pa smiled.

I sat down at the table.

"Let's say grace." Pa bowed his head.

Beth Ann and I closed our eyes and bowed our heads. Today was just like any other day, but my heart was racing. There was one thing different about today. Today Luke was coming. I tried not to think about it, but every other thought was about Luke and the differences he would bring to my life.

"Lord, please look after our Lucy. Please bless her marriage to Mr. Larson and help them find happiness. Thank you for the food and the hands that prepared it. We thank you for having good weather on the farm this year and we pray we have good weather next year too, in Jesus' name; amen." Pa finished.

"Amen." Beth Ann and I echoed.

The three of us finished up breakfast. I made my way outside and got the wagon ready while Beth Ann finished the dishes. I pulled the wagon as close to the house as I could manage, so Pa wouldn't have to walk as far.

"Come on, Pa." I held the front door open.

Pa walked out the door.

"Are you wearing that?" My sister was appalled.

"Yes, that's why I have it on." I rolled my eyes.

"Lucy, for once in your life, put on a dress!" My sister ran after me.

I turned on my heels. "Dresses are no good for a farm."

"It isn't for a workday. It's for your wedding day." My sister put her hand on her hip.

"Better not to let him get the wrong idea." I helped Pa climb into the wagon.

Pa chuckled softly.

"Are you comfortable?" I covered my Pa up with a quilt.

I felt bad for taking him to town on the bumpy road. It wasn't good for his leg. I knew getting married was important, but there wasn't any reason to destroy your leg just to go to a wedding.

"I'm not missing my little girl's wedding." Pa's blue eye steeled on my face.

"I'm not a little girl no more, Pa." I rolled my eyes.

"Beth Ann, tie up Lucy's horse to the wagon." Pa instructed.

"Pa." I complained.

Beth Ann closed the door to the house and walked to the barn. A few minutes later, she was tying Daisy to the wagon. I knew where this was going, and I didn't like it. I hopped into the wagon. Beth Ann hopped up in the wagon and covered herself up with a quilt.

"This wagon is going to be full; besides, you might want to have some alone time with your groom." Pa told me.

I ignored my Pa and flicked the reins. Beth Ann chattered all the way to town. It helped drown out all of the questions running through my mind.

What kind of man would relocate his life to marry a strange woman? I wouldn't leave the family farm for anyone. Luke was bringing his brother and Ma, so something must have happened to his Pa. I wonder what happened to Luke's Pa?

I knew what it was like to be without a Ma. My heart hurt thinking about her. I rubbed the chain around my neck. It used to be Ma's necklace. I missed her a lot, especially today.

I tried to imagine how I would feel if the roles were reversed. I'd always been more of a Daddy's girl. If my Pa wasn't around, we would have lost the farm a long time ago. If I didn't have the farm, life would be different. I heard a train whistle in the distance. I guess I was about to find out what kind of man I was marrying.

Luke

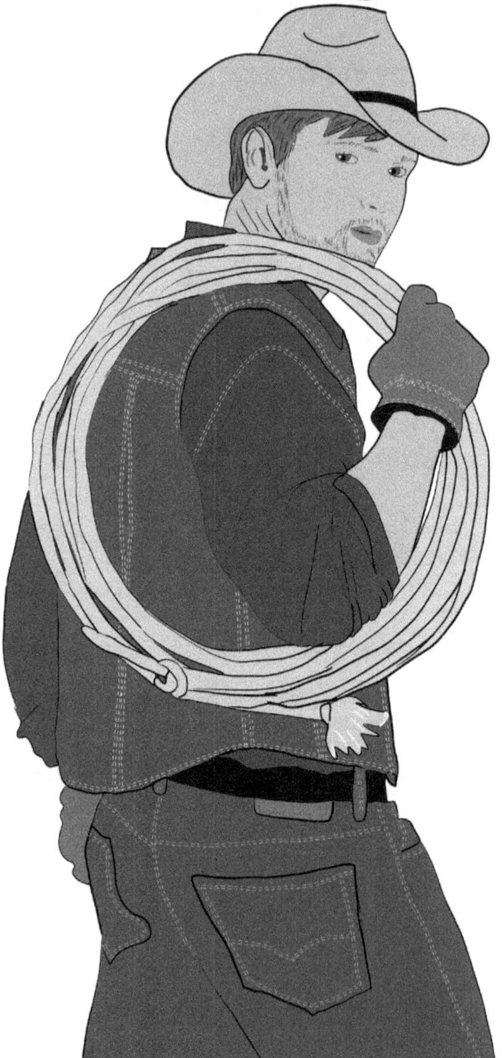

Six

6

I stepped down off the train. Everything we had fit in two carpet bags and a trunk. Tommy followed me over to the baggage area. I handed him both bags. He frowned at me, but said nothing. I picked up the trunk and sat it down on the edge of the building.

A wagon pulled up with an older man, and a young girl in the back of the wagon. In the front of the wagon, was a figure wearing pants and a stetson. She did her best to hide it, but the curves of her hips and chest were unmistakable. She was definitely a woman.

The woman in the stetson hopped down from the wagon like a woman in charge. She tied the horses to the post and turned her face my way. I had never seen beautiful blue eyes on such a striking face before. A strand of strawberry blonde hair escaped her hat. Those blue eyes landed on me.

"Luke, is that her?" Tommy whistled.

The woman's blue eyes landed on my kid brother.

"Tommy." I growled.

"Sorry, she's just really pretty, even if she isn't wearing a dress." Tommy hissed back.

I walked towards the woman. "I'm Luke Larson." I took my hat off my head. It seemed like the sort of thing to do when you were supposed to be marrying her.

"Lucy Dawson." The beautiful woman's tone was stern.

Lucy nodded her head once to me. I could feel her eyes examining me. I was sure it was some kind of test. Since we traveled all this way, I hoped I passed.

"This is my Pa and my sister, Beth Ann." She nodded toward the wagon.

"Pleasure to meet you, Mr. Dawson. Miss Dawson." I nodded at each of them.

Beth Ann giggled. "He's handsome."

Lucy sent a look of daggers at her sister as blood rushed to my face. The only one who called me handsome was my Ma. I didn't really think that counted. I was pretty sure all mothers said that kind of stuff to their sons.

"This is my Ma." I pointed at my mother. "And my brother, Tommy." I nodded towards my brother.

Lucy paused and took each of them in as if she were mulling over something. "Nice to meet you, Mrs. Larson. Mr. Larson." She glanced at my mother and then at my brother.

Beth Ann giggled again.

"Mr. Larson, you can put your stuff in the back of the wagon." Lucy's Pa told me.

"Yes, sir." I put my hat back on.

I gave a pointed look at my brother, who actually followed my lead without kicking up a fit like normal. The two of us picked up the trunk and put it in the wagon beside Mr. Dawson. Tommy picked up a bag and put it in the wagon. I picked up the last bag and put it in.

"We best get to it." Lucy glanced at me.

I nodded once. I was too struck by her beauty to say more than I had to. I wanted to make a good impression.

Lucy untied the horses and gave the reins to her sister. I helped Ma into the wagon. I wasn't sure if we would all fit in the wagon. With the trunk, it was kind of crowded. Tommy hopped into the wagon and sat on the trunk.

"I'm walking over." Lucy pointed at the church.

"I'll walk with you." I held Miss Dawson's eyes.

Lucy was unusually quiet, but seemed to have a storm going behind those baby blues. I was pretty sure women were supposed to talk a lot, at least all of the women I'd been around did. She finally nodded and walked over with me.

The woman I was betrothed to walked straight to the house beside the church and knocked on the door. The door flew open. A short man stood in front of us. He peered at Lucy.

"We're ready to get hitched." Lucy told the man who opened the door.

"Alright then." The pastor smiled. "Mary! Miss Dawson is finally getting hitched."

"I'm coming." A plump woman hurried to his side. Two little ones clung to her legs.

The word finally brought a flash of concern. 22 was considered an old maid where I came from, but Lucy didn't look like an old maid to me. She definitely had a mind of her own, but a strong-willed woman didn't scare me; getting married to one I just met did.

"Pa broke his leg, so we'd like to have the ceremony by the wagon." Lucy stood straighter.

"That's fine. Let me get my Bible." The preacher disappeared into the house.

Lucy glanced at me.

Should I smile? My stomach tightened. My breakfast better stay down.

I forced myself to breathe evenly. I could do this. Marrying Lucy was the plan. This was either going to be the best decision of my life, or the worst.

Lucy

Seven

7

"Let's go wait by the wagon." I motioned back towards my Pa.

"Okay." Luke nodded.

My sister jumped out of the wagon. I wasn't sure what she was up to as she started running around the yard. I opted to ignore her.

"The Preacher will be right out." I put my arm on the wagon.

"I'll be here." My Pa gave me a nod of encouragement.

"You really want to marrying my brother?" Tommy's eyes were wide.

"Shh." Mrs. Larson silenced her youngest son.

"Sorry, Ma. I was just asking." Tommy was contrite.

Children flew out of the parsonage. The Preacher came walking towards us with his wife. He stopped in front of the wagon. He opened the Bible to a marked page.

"Are you both ready?" The Preacher's gaze landed on me.

I nodded.

The Preacher turned to the man I was about to marry.

"Yes, sir." Mr. Larson nodded.

"Wait!" Beth Ann ran over.

I scowled at my sister. What was she doing? I didn't expect her to break up my wedding.

"Lucy!" Beth Ann put a bouquet of flowers in my hand.

"What are you doing?" I demanded.

"You wouldn't wear a dress. The least you could do is hold some flowers." Beth Ann growled.

"Beth Ann..." I wasn't the kind of woman who cared about flowers.

"Ma would have wanted you to have flowers. Tell her Pa." Beth Ann put a hand on her hip.

Pa cleared his throat. "Your Ma had flowers at our wedding."

"Thank you for the flowers, Beth Ann." I held them against my will.

I couldn't resist the urge to glance at the man I was about to marry. A slight smile was in the corner of Mr. Larson's lips. My stomach tightened like it never had in my life. Beth Ann was right; he was a handsome man. Surely, he could have found someone to marry back home. He didn't have a Pa, maybe that's why he agreed to this arrangement. At least he had been honest about bringing his brother and Ma with him.

I was considered an old maid around here, but it's hard to settle for a man you can out shoot, outride, and out think. What's the point in settling for...?

"Repeat after me. I, Lucy..." The Preacher began.

I was having a hard time thinking as I repeated after the Preacher. I kept glancing at Luke Larson. He was a mighty handsome man. I don't know what I expected, but the bulging muscles underneath his slender shirt weren't it. I'm not sure I've seen a bet-ter-looking man in my life. I swallowed.

"I do." I finished.

Luke's brown eyes were soulful as he vowed to love and cherish me... the to have and to hold part made it hard not to look at his strong forearms and biceps.

I need help on the ranch; I reminded myself. He needs a place to live. This was an arrangement.

My thoughts drifted to the other side of the fence. It may be an arrangement, but it was a marriage. This was forever.

"I do." Luke finished.

"You may kiss the bride." The Preacher informed us.

Luke's eyes turned nervous. I was too. I nodded once at Luke. He took off his hat and covered my lips with his. It was over quickly. I wasn't sure what to make of this man who was now my husband.

Luke bent down and retrieved my hat. He handed it to me. I didn't realize that it fell off. I carefully took it.

Luke was staring at me differently. I wasn't sure why. That's when my hair picked up in the wind. I bent down and tucked my hair back in my hat.

Luke

Eight
8

I hadn't realized just how beautiful Lucy was until her hair cascaded across her shoulders. On top of all that, she was my wife. A sense of responsibility landed on my shoulders. I wanted to protect this woman in front of me with my life. I have never felt something this intense so quickly. I wanted to be her everything.

There were cheers and hoots from our family. I smiled and nodded at them. Lucy's opinion was the one that mattered to me. Was she happy that I answered her ad?

"Lucy, why don't you take your husband home? We'll be on our way after a bit." My new father-in-law instructed.

Lucy glanced at me and said nothing as she untied the horse tied to the wagon. I couldn't take my eyes off of her. She was deliberate in every move she made. She climbed onto the saddle.

My wife's blazing blue eyes held a challenge in them. I climbed up behind her with ease. I had ridden with Tommy like this before, but this was the first time I had been close to any woman besides my Ma.

My thoughts flew faster than they ever had. I prized myself in being a fairly composed man, but the way I was feeling sitting this close to Lucy... was not first meeting kind of thoughts. The only thing I had to hold on to was her. It seemed wrong with her Pa right there and the Preacher watching.

I couldn't see a way of getting around holding her without falling off the horse. I put my right arm around her dainty waist. I felt her back stiffen slightly as she flicked the reins. I put my left hand around the other side of her. When we were out of town, her back relaxed slightly.

"Are you comfortable?" She tilted her head slightly towards me.

Comfortable, absolutely not. She was driving me crazy. Lucy didn't seem to have any idea what she was doing to me. I was trying to give her as much space as I could and still stay on the horse. It wasn't easy. Ma and Pa had drilled into me that I was to treat women with respect and holding a woman this close on a horse hadn't come up. I was doing my best not to touch anything I shouldn't.

"No." My voice came out stronger than it felt.

"Well, it's a long ride and it will be a longer one if you fall off." Lucy countered.

I decided that was her way of giving me permission to hold her, so I scooted closer. Her back melted against my chest. I wrapped my hands around her dainty waist. It felt like she was meant to be there. Lucy paused a moment and took off at a faster speed. My mind shouldn't have had time to wander... but it did.

We hit a bump, and my hands shifted. I moved my hand back to a more appropriate place. Lucy was my wife, but I hadn't thought past too much more than providing a place for Ma and Tommy to sleep. What kind of husband was Lucy expecting me to be? I swallowed.

Pa had seemed like a good husband to Ma. I wanted to be a good husband to Lucy. She needed a man to help her out on the farm, so I vowed to myself to be that man. I didn't mind hard work. I promised myself that I would be a man that Lucy would be proud to call her husband.

"This is the property line." Lucy called over her shoulder.

I kind of wish the ride out to Lucy's farm was a little longer. I held Lucy tighter. I knew my reason to hold her close was coming to an end.

Lucy

Nine
9

"This is the barn." I took care of Daisy and put her in her stall with some food and water.

"It's nice." Luke was examining the barn.

When I glanced at Luke, he seemed to mean it. I don't know why it mattered so much if he liked the barn or not. Maybe because the barn was a reflection of who I was as a person?

I pushed away the deep thoughts. Right now, I was giving Luke the tour. The problem was that Luke was more than just a man to me; he was my husband. He was the man I was about to spend my life with.

"That's the main house." I pointed. "Behind it is the outside kitchen. Your Ma will be in there with Tommy." Beth Ann and I have worked hard to get it ready in time.

"Thank you." Luke's voice was so quiet that I barely heard him.

I turned toward him. His dark eyes were sincere. I nodded. I hadn't expected to like Luke. I knew I couldn't run this farm full time by myself. With Pa down for a while and him getting older, I needed a husband to share the load.

I continued walking further away from the main house. Luke kept up with me easily. I stopped in front of the one roomed building. I glanced at Luke and opened the door. He stepped in after me and took off his hat nervously.

The room seemed much smaller with him standing here. On the bed was a basket. I walked over. That's when I vaguely remembered Beth Ann running in here before we went into town.

"Are you hungry?" I glanced over my shoulder.

Luke nodded.

I sat down on the bed. Then it felt uncomfortable, so I stood up. I haven't been this wound up since I was a child.

"We should pray." He motioned towards the food.

I took off my hat. My blonde hair fell around my neck. Luke's eyes met mine. He held out his hand to me. I paused for a moment before taking it. I wasn't used to holding any man's hand beside my Pa's hand during prayer at mealtime.

This man had a surprising presence about him. Holding his hand was nothing like holding Pa's or Beth Ann's hand. It may sound strange, but I already felt like we were a team.

"Lord, thank you for bringing me and my family here safely. Thank you for your provision, including the meal before us. Thank you for my new wife. Help us to have a strong marriage. In Jesus' name, amen." Luke squeezed my hand slightly and let go.

I reached to put my hat back on my head.

"I'd rather you not." Luke's tone was firm.

I paused. He was staring at me like I was... pretty. I swallowed and put the hat on the rack by the door. Luke handed me his, and I hung it up as well. When I turned around, he was putting a blanket on the ground.

"I haven't had a picnic in a spell." His eyes met mine.

Why was he looking at me like that? He barely knew me. My new husband turned around and put the basket on the blanket. He lowered himself down and patted the spot next to him.

We both divided up the food and ate in silence for a few minutes. The silence felt uncomfortable. Beth Ann was good at jawing. I didn't usually have to worry about keeping up a conversation.

"Thank you for coming." I finally spoke.

Luke froze. "I'm glad I saw the advertisement first." He had a slight smile in the corner of his mouth.

"You didn't." I swallowed.

This must have come as news to him, because his eyes were wide.

"What made you pick me?" Luke put his arm on the bed and turned towards me.

"Yours was the only one that sounded... like a good fit." I thought that would be enough of an answer, but Luke waited for me to elaborate. "One of them wanted me to be a Ma to eight children and move in with him."

Luke's eyes were wide.

"I threw it away. One of them wanted me to send him money to come here, which would have been alright, but he asked for enough to build a house and buy a large patch of land." I continued.

"I see." Luke's eyes clouded.

I felt bad, but I didn't know why. "For what it's worth, I'm glad you came."

My new husband's eyes softened. "Me too."

Luke was easy to be around. Most men looked at me like I was a hurdle to cross. Luke looked at me like I was a woman. Being with him was like almost touching a burning poker without actually touching it. I've never wanted to play with fire so badly in my life.

"I'm glad I had the right answers." Luke's smile was downright handsome.

I couldn't help laughing. Luke was watching me as if I were an angel. I've never had a boy look at me like that.

"Enough of them." I couldn't help smiling. I noticed Luke staring at my lips. "What?"

"I'd very much like to kiss you again, Mrs. Larson." Luke's deep voice shook me to my core.

The thought of kissing Luke again had me warm all over. When he had his arms around me on the ride back home, it was all I had been able to think about.

"I reckon that'd be okay." I finally spoke.

Anticipation flooded through my veins. Luke place a short kiss on my lips. Then another. The third was longer. He pulled back and our eyes met. The air between us was on fire.

Luke's eyes didn't leave my face. I hated to admit it, but I liked Luke's kisses a little too much. We had an hour before the ranch would be full of prying eyes.

"I'd like to do that again." I admitted.

Luke didn't budge for a second as if he was taking in the situation. Then he moved closer to me. His hand went to my cheek. I couldn't remember the last time my cheek had been touched by anyone other than me or my horse. I touched his face in return. I felt drawn to Luke like I had never been drawn to another man in my life.

Our lips touched. This time was longer than the other kisses combined. I pulled him closer. He was happy to oblige.

"Is that alright?" My husband pulled back slightly.

I nodded my head. Maybe there was something to this marriage thing. Luke's face was flushed.

"Are you too hot in here?" I frowned. "I can open the window."

Luke shook his head. "It's my beautiful wife that's..." He stopped.

"Beautiful?" I was unsure of his assessment.

"You're the prettiest woman I've laid my eyes on." Luke brushed a stray hair behind my ear.

I was feeling a little flushed myself. "Thank you." I licked my bottom lip. "I didn't expect you to be handsome."

Luke eyed me curiously. "I didn't expect you to be so pretty. I guess we both had a surprise." A smile twitched on his lips.

Luke

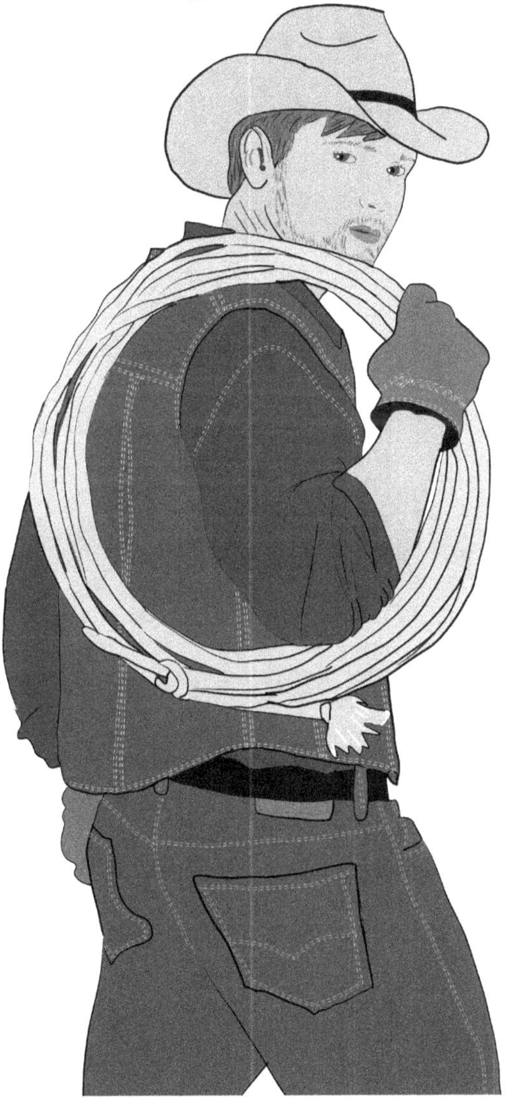

Ten
10

My eyes flew open as soft hair brushed over my bare shoulder. I woke up with someone in my bed. Lucy.

I was with Lucy. The fog cleared slightly in my head. I yawned, and she rolled over and snuggled closer. Her hand fell across my stomach. I froze. I gently put my arm around her and she mumbled something in her sleep that I couldn't understand.

This woman was my wife. It was my responsibility to make sure she was happy and healthy. I wasn't able to add anything to our marriage, but me. I really hoped that was enough.

I had a hard time falling asleep last night. When I did, my thoughts were filled with a beautiful blue-eyed woman with cascading blonde hair. I laid in bed holding

Lucy. I didn't want to leave, but I knew morning chores needed to be done.

I carefully got out of bed and got dressed. I paused and stared at my wife. I was a lucky man, and I wanted to do everything in my power to make her feel like marrying me was the right decision.

I wish I had all the money in the world to spoil her, but I didn't. I was young and strong. It was time I proved to Lucy and myself that I was up for the challenge of being her husband.

I carefully opened the door and stepped outside. By some miracle, I didn't wake her. It was still dark out. I blew on my hands to warm them up.

I remember seeing some lanterns in the barn yesterday. I found them hanging on the wall beside of the door. On the ledge behind the lanterns, was a box of matches. I picked the matches up and managed to light one. The animals started moving around. They knew it was chow time.

I lit the lantern and put the matches back on the ledge. I could see my breath. Winter was coming soon. I'd only been here a day, so I wasn't sure if they needed more wood. Lucy seemed pretty sensible. They probably had enough food around here in a cellar somewhere.

I was a decent hunter. Tommy and I could go deer hunting. That would put meat on the table. Knowing Lucy, she was probably good at that too.

I was determined to keep up with my wife when it came to sharing the load of work. A woman that would rather wear men's clothing than dresses had to be a woman full of fire. My cheeks heated when I thought about the fire she had been last night.

"First things first." I walked towards the animals. "My name is Luke Larson. I'm going to be around this here barn every day. You best get used to me now."

The animals were starting to come toward me.

"I know." I started with feeding the chickens.

I found a pail and went outside of the barn and pumped some water to feed the chickens. I pumped more water and finished watering the other animals. I fed all the animals that needed fed and decided it was time to start milking the cows.

I found the milking stool. A pail was beside it. I looked inside. It looked clean. I brought the first cow out of the stall. She was a good cow. I sat down to start milking her. I blew on my hand so they would be warm.

"I'm Luke. Would you like me to sing you a song?" I patted the side of the cow.

The cow gave a soft moo. She didn't seem to mind that I was new around here. I blew on my hands again. When I was done milking her, I put her back in her stall and got out the next cow.

Lucy

Eleven
11

"I wish I knew what to call you, girl." Luke cooed as he sat on the stool. He patted my cow on her side. He blew on his hands to warm them and started filling the pail.

There was a hint of a sunrise in the distance, but it hadn't quite made up its mind yet. I was sure Luke would have said something if he saw me coming, but he didn't. I took the moment to examine my new husband. It was rare that anyone woke up before me. I instantly had a better opinion of him.

My thoughts flashed to last night. The cold didn't seem nearly as cold. So far, my new husband had been a surprise in every way imaginable.

Luke started singing quietly to my cow. He had an attractive tone in his voice. Something about Luke drew me in. A twig snapped under my foot.

Luke stopped singing and glanced over his shoulder. He saw me. An instant smile lit up his face.

Something about the way the man in front of me smiled at me, kissed me, and touched me made me feel like more of a woman than I have in my entire life.

I was used to waking up before dawn, putting in an hour or two before breakfast. After breakfast, I'd put in several more hours. There never seemed to be enough time in the day to get it all done. Now Luke was here to help.

"Good morning, Lucy." His dark eyes were warm.

Moo! My cow was upset. I wasn't sure if it was because he had stopped singing or if she didn't want to wait anymore.

"Sorry, girl." Luke rubbed her side.

"Rosie." I stepped closer.

"Good girl, Rosie." Luke started milking her again. I heard the steady rhythm of the milk pail being filled.

"Did you sleep well?" I hesitated.

Luke stopped. His warm brown eyes met mine. A soft smile covered his lips. I blushed slightly and turned around. I walked over to check the horses. They had already been fed.

I turned my head sharply. "You fed the animals."

"I did." Luke's warm voice was amused.

"And you sing?" I wasn't used to having my chores done before I woke up.

"I do." Luke glanced over his shoulder at me again. "Do you?"

I shook my head no.

Luke rubbed Rosie's side. "Good girl." He whispered before standing up. I watched my husband put Rosie back in her stall. He walked over to me. "Anything else you need me to do?"

I found myself staring at his lips. Luke's smile grew. Apparently, I hadn't been subtle. He stepped closer. His lips covered mine. My hands wrapped around his neck. I felt his large arms wrap around me and pull me closer. Kissing Luke was... perfect. When his lips left mine, he tucked a stray hair behind my ear.

"Good morning, Lucy." Luke gave me a quick peck on the lips.

"You already said that." I mumbled.

Luke smiled. "I like saying it."

I had a feeling he liked the kissing part. The problem was I did too. Everything with Luke was new. It felt like we were on a journey together.

"Do you want me to say it again?" Luke's dark eyes were teasing.

I giggled.

Luke smiled at me. "I love your laugh."

"Are you trying to charm me, Luke Larson?" I stepped closer to my husband.

"That depends. Is it working?" Luke's warm breath brushed my face.

"Maybe a little? Why don't you tell me good morning again?" I couldn't believe I was being so brazen with him.

"Good morning, Mrs. Larson." Luke bent down and kissed me again.

Luke

Twelve
12

I couldn't help smiling. My beautiful wife had a nice stain on her cheeks and I was the one that put it there. I planned to do it every chance I got.

"I reckon I could help with breakfast since all of my morning chores are done." Lucy's brilliant blue eyes were watching me carefully. "Then I'll..."

"We'll." I interrupted her.

I had a feeling she was used to doing everything alone. I wasn't about to let my woman keep that up. I came here for her and my kin. Lucy was my kin now, and I was going to lighten the load on her.

"You sent for me to help, remember?" My voice sounded deep to my own ears.

Sometimes I opened my mouth and was surprised a man came out. Other times, I wish I was a little older so everyone else wouldn't act like I was a young buck with no direction. I would do everything within my power to make this marriage work with Lucy.

Lucy nodded. "I reckon you can help muck out the stalls." She sent me a sly grin.

"Actually, I think Tommy should do that... him being the youngest and all." Tommy wasn't that young, but I was his older brother. What good was being the oldest, if I couldn't boss him around sometime?

As I stared at my wife, I realized I wasn't the oldest around her. Somehow, the thought of her bossing me around made me want to kiss her. I was looking forward to shut eye even though the day had just begun, and I knew that had everything to do with my beautiful head-strong wife.

"Alright, so what am I supposed to do with all this free time on my hands? Because you're not going to stick me in the kitchen to cook and clean for you all the time." Lucy pointed at the main house.

She didn't sound happy. I wasn't sure why, but the only thing I could think of was being close to her. Beth Ann said something yesterday about Lucy not liking to work inside. I had a feeling she might be riled up about being cooped up in the house. If my wife was going to be riled up, I didn't want her to be cantankerous at me.

I stepped closer. "Wouldn't dream of it." I mumbled against her lips as I kissed her. She met my kiss like it had been her idea. "You're perfect." I breathed when I let her go.

Lucy's eyes were full of something I couldn't define, but I liked whatever it was.

"I was thinking that a better use of your time would be to show me the property line and tell me what you envisioned for this place. Unless you prefer mucking out stalls." I smirked.

Lucy licked her bottom lip and shook her head no. She was too quiet. I wasn't sure why.

"Did I do something wrong?" I was doing my best not to screw this marriage up.

"No." Lucy shook her head slightly.

"Something seems off." I took off my hat and ran my fingers through my hair and put my hat back on.

"Luke, what kind of wife are you expecting me to be?" Lucy's voice was barely audible.

"Expecting?" I was confused.

Lucy nodded.

Whatever was going on in Lucy's head seemed to need some jawing from me. I prayed I said the right thing. It might be easier to say the right thing if I knew what the issue was. Apparently, it was something.

"I'm trying to figure this out." I paused. "I thought you wanted me to come out here and help with the farm, and be a husband to you."

Lucy nodded.

"So, that's what I'm doing." I continued. I racked my brain for what went wrong and then what Beth Ann mentioned yesterday popped up in my memories. "Are you upset cause you think I want you in the kitchen just cause I tried to help with the chores?"

Lucy licked her bottom lip again.

That must be the issue, cause I was sure she would have denied it by now. I had to fix this and fix it now. The problem was the only thing on my mind was touching her and being close to her.

"Look Lucy." I stepped closer. "How I see it is that Ma cooks fine. She likes being in a kitchen. Always has.

Beth Ann said she was doing the cooking before Ma came. That's two cooks in a kitchen. I don't think they need a third cook in the kitchen, unless you want to be in there."

Lucy shook her head no.

"I want to make this work. You're the handsomest woman I've ever seen. The barn was immaculate. Whatever you set your heart on doing, I say you do that." I swallowed and prayed those were the right words. With Lucy, it was hard to tell.

Lucy threw her arms around me so hard that she knocked me back a few steps. I wrapped my arms around her. This was where this woman was meant to be. I don't know how God made her so perfect, but I think my lucky stars he did.

"Glad that's settled." I grinned.

"Me too." Lucy smiled shyly.

The rooster started crowing at the new day. A moment later, the door opened and Beth Ann came outside. She didn't see us inside of the barn.

"Should I have gotten the eggs?" I kept my voice low, so Beth Ann wouldn't hear me.

"Beth Ann's chore is to get the eggs for breakfast." Lucy whispered.

Beth Ann rushed back inside of the house without seeing us.

"How long should we hide out here until breakfast is ready?" I leaned on the beam in the middle of the barn.

"Five minutes." Lucy stepped closer to me.

"Any ideas what we can do with five minutes?" I grinned.

"A few." Lucy returned my smile.

Lucy

Thirteen
13

I kept stealing glances at Luke during breakfast. He was fairly self-assured. I wasn't sure why he felt he needed to come out here to find a wife, but I liked that he wasn't set on me being in the kitchen. When he took over my chores this morning, I was concerned he was trying to take my job from me.

"Tommy, when breakfast is over, I need you to muck out the stalls." Luke told his brother.

Tommy made a face, but nodded.

"Is Tommy coming with me to school today?" Beth Ann leaned forward.

Tommy shifted his gaze from Luke to his Ma. She nodded. Tommy grinned. I think he was just trying to get out of chores. I've never had a younger brother before, but I expect they have a lot in common with younger sisters. Beth Ann liked having her own way too.

"You'll have plenty of time to muck out the stalls before you go." Luke's stare was hard.

Tommy made another face.

"I'll help. It won't take long." Beth Ann smiled.

She usually helped me out most mornings, so it wasn't out of the ordinary for her to be in the barn.

"Okay." Tommy beamed.

"Lucy's going to show me the property after breakfast." Luke's eyes met mine.

"That's a good idea." Pa spoke up.

Pa seemed pleased to have Luke around. Truthfully, I knew Pa always wanted a boy. Now, with Luke and Tommy around, it was like he had gotten two sons for the price of one.

"I will make you lunches." Luke's Ma offered.

"Thanks, Ma." My husband smiled. He had a glimmer in his eyes when his gaze returned to me.

I wasn't used to this much dividing of the labor. Beth Ann and I usually took turns with the cooking and washing dishes. I hated every minute of being indoors, so I usually wiggled out of doing dishes any chance I got. Beth Ann helped me out in the barn in the mornings, but she preferred to stay inside.

Now, Luke's Ma was cooking, which meant I was free of that chore. Luke was having Tommy muck out the stalls, so I was free of that chore. My husband thought it was a good idea to let me sleep in and feed the animals.

This new way of doing things had me on edge. Or maybe it was Luke? It was hard to know the difference with so many new things going on.

Pa was usually a reigning force, but this accident had done something I hadn't expected. He'd practical- ly handed the land over to me. He strongly suggested I find a husband to help with it, because he wouldn't be around forever.

I had chewed on it for a few days and decided finding a husband was the best solution. I couldn't run this place by myself. As it was, the three of us had been struggling for some time. Three extra hands would be extra mouths to feed, but the added help made it worth it.

"I don't want to step on any toes, but if it's okay with you fine people, I'm used to earning my keep in the kitchen." Luke's Ma spoke up.

"Ma's a real good cook." Tommy spoke between bites.

"She is." Luke's warm gaze fell on me.

"That suits me fine." I muttered before taking a drink.

"Lucy hates kitchen work." Beth Ann teased.

"I'm needed outside more." I gave my sister a glare.

"I'm sure you are." Luke's dark eyes were warm.

Luke hadn't taken over the house, but his presence was felt immediately. It was nice. The chores didn't seem overwhelming like they did when Pa first got hurt.

"Lucy's always liked being outdoors." Pa smiled at me proudly. "She's my little tomboy."

I nodded and smiled slightly.

"Luke, what do you think about your wife being a tomboy?" Tommy took a drink from his cup.

I turned to my husband. I was very interested in his answer. Luke froze mid bite and glanced around the table. He put his fork down.

"I think Lucy is fine how she is." Luke's smile was endearing. "And I think you need to learn to shut your yap." He shot his brother a stern look.

"Sorry." Tommy winced.

"Lucy's been called way worse." Beth Ann confided.

"Beth Ann!" I glared at my sister.

"What? You have." Beth Ann made a face at me.

I could throttle her right now.

I felt a hand on my leg under the table before I could say something to my sister. I glanced over at Luke. He was amused, but I knew in my heart that he was here for me.

"If you keep jawing, you're both going to be late for school." Pa spoke up.

"Sorry, Pa." Beth Ann put a forkful in her mouth.

"Yeah, we don't want to be late." Tommy finished his food.

"You're just trying to get out of chores." Luke's tone deepened.

Luke

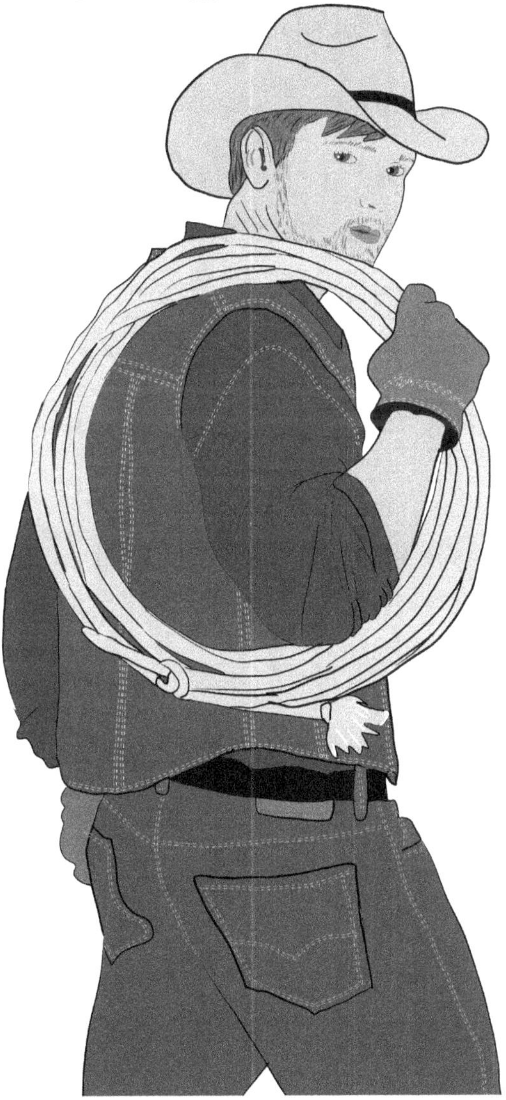

Fourteen
14

I followed a little behind Lucy, not that I couldn't keep up, but because of the view. She rode her horse like a woman on a mission. My wife was strong and fierce, but when she stood next to me, a fierce desire to protect her took over. I wanted to be the man she needed, but first I had to figure out what that was.

Lucy slowed down. "Are you coming?"

I smiled. "Just taking in the view."

Lucy cocked an eyebrow, but didn't comment.

"This part of the property doesn't look like it's being worked." I pointed. "Off year?"

"Yes, and no." She pointed behind us. "We usually alternate that field and this one with corn and soybeans. We have the family garden closer to the house." Lucy pointed behind us. "But this field is empty, because it's too much for us to work with just me and Pa."

We had come to a slow walk. I licked my bottom lip and examined the field and thought about what we had just passed. It was a lot of work, but it wasn't overgrown yet. Winter wasn't too far away. This would be a project for the spring.

"I'm here now." My eyes turned to my new wife. "We'll work this field next spring too."

Lucy's eyebrows raised. "Okay, Luke."

We rode a little further. The land was beautiful. I was in love instantly.

There was so much to do. The further we rode, the more land I saw that had gone by the wayside. I had a hard time understanding why all of this land wasn't being worked. It was a big property, which meant more money for the family if it had been worked.

"Why haven't you hired a few hands to help out?" I finally asked.

Lucy shifted uncomfortably in her seat. "When Ma died, I was responsible for Beth Ann." She paused.

I waited for her to continue.

"We had someone... two of them, but they... tried to... well, I had to take the shotgun from behind the door and scare them off. Pa heard and... they were let go." Lucy's blue eyes were troubled.

"You should have shot them." I felt anger in the pit of my stomach. Hatred boiled up in my stomach for my wife. I had never felt like shooting anyone in my life, until today.

Lucy's blue eyes caught mine. "The gun wasn't loaded. We keep the shells behind the door, so they didn't know any different."

I gritted my teeth. "They ain't around town anymore, are they?"

Lucy shook her beautiful blonde head as some stray hairs came out. "They moved on."

I nodded. We were both quiet for a moment. My eyes kept flickering to the property line closer to the trees. I could imagine a home there. Lucy, me... and babies. I wonder if Lucy even wanted children. I thought about it. I could see her having a baby on the saddle with her.

"What do you think about a house there?" I pointed.

Lucy's head followed the direction of my hand and back. Her eyes were guarded, but curious. "What did you have in mind?"

We rode closer. I got off my horse and tied him to a tree. Lucy did the same. She seemed so much smaller walking beside me.

"The main room could be here." I pointed. "With a fireplace." I met her gaze. She seemed to be listening to my every word. "We would have to put in a water pump." I put my hand on my hips.

"There are lots of springs around here." Lucy spoke up.

"So it shouldn't be too hard to run into water." I smiled.

"I wouldn't think so." She agreed.

"This could be our room." I pointed at an area of the property.

I saw a blush beginning on Lucy's cheeks.

"Maybe we could put a fireplace in here too?" I smiled.

"I'd like that." Lucy's voice was soft.

"And an extra room here." I paused. "Just in case."
I turned around.

"Just in case?" Lucy's eyes were warm.

I stepped closer. "Yeah."

I wanted to kiss her. From the look in her eyes, she could feel it too. I bent down my head and our lips met.

"What do you think, Sweetheart?" It was the first time I called her that and from the sharp look in her eyes, she noticed.

"I think we have a lot to do this spring." She put her smaller hand on my forearm.

I couldn't help smiling. I felt a bond with Lucy, even though we had only known each other for a short while.

"Can I ask you something?" Lucy's voice was uneasy.

"Anything." I stepped closer to her.

"Why did you come out here... you're a good-looking man... you could have...?" She stopped for a moment. "Why'd you marry me?"

"So... you think I'm good-looking?" I grinned.

She mentioned something about me being hand-some earlier in the barn, but this time, I took her more seriously. She came across as bashful when she said it, which had to be the cutest thing in the whole state. I've never cared much about how I looked until Lucy mentioned she liked how I looked. I wanted my wife to like me.

Lucy's cheeks were pink again. "I'm sure it's not the first time you've been told that."

"True, but my Ma says the same thing to Tommy." I was still grinning like a fool.

Lucy chuckled. "Well..."

"Pa died, and the work dried up back home. I hap-pened on your advertisement when I went to check for a job posting. I'd been checking every day for weeks with no luck. You sounded like... a sensible woman and it was an opportunity to take care of my family."

"Oh." Her eyes were slightly downcast.

I put my hand under her chin and lifted it to mine. "I'm glad I answered it."

"You are?" Her skin was softer than I imagined.

I nodded. "What about you?"

Lucy swallowed. "It seemed like a logical choice."

"How so?" I let my hand fall away.

"I'm not exactly easy to get along with. Pa calls me strong-willed. Beth Ann says I'm stubborn." Lucy was having a hard time meeting my gaze when she talked about herself.

"I like a challenge." It wasn't lost on me that this would be our bedroom if I had my way.

"Me too." Lucy smiled back.

I slid my hand in hers as we walked back to the horses.

"Luke?" Her voice was more delicate than I expected.

"Yes?"

"Thank you for coming." Lucy glanced at me.

I gave her hand a slight squeeze. "I think I'm going to like being married to you, Lucy Larson."

"Good thing, it's a little too late to be changing your mind." She had the beginnings of a smile on her lips.

I busted out laughing. "Give me your honest opinion, are you okay if we build a house out here?"

Lucy paused and scanned the area. "I am. It will be a lot of hard work."

"Tommy will help. I think we can finish it up by late spring." I nodded.

"You have been here one day and already have a list two miles wide." Lucy grinned.

"I told you I came to work." I flashed her a smile as I climbed up on my horse. "Race you back?"

"Get ready to lose." A large smile spread across my wife's face.

I chuckled. I had a feeling that either way, I wouldn't be losing. Lucy urged her horse ahead of me and I hurried to catch up.

Lucy

Fifteen
15

I heard a steady rhythm behind the house. It sounded like someone was cutting firewood. Pa wasn't up for it. My sister avoided that chore every chance she could. She hated splinters. It usually fell on me. I didn't mind, but it wasn't my favorite chore.

I rounded the corner to see a well-defined back staring back at me. The ax went above his head and came down. He moved the wood and repeated the action and picked up another piece of wood and did the same. He left the ax in the tree stump as he bent down to gather the wood.

"Need some help?" I stepped closer.

Luke smiled. "Shore."

I bent down and filled my arms with wood and put them on the woodpile. Luke put his large pile beside mine. A few were out of place, so I pushed them in.

When we went to gather more wood, our hands touched. My eyes met his. There was an undefined glimmer in them that I couldn't place. A slow smile curved on his lips. We put the rest of the wood on the pile. I readjusted them again. Luke leaned against the pile slightly.

"Where's your shirt?" I couldn't help myself from asking.

Luke smiled and gestured to the ground. "No use getting it dirty cutting wood."

"So you're just getting yourself dirty instead?" I gestured to a small sliver of wood on his side.

Luke's eyes traveled down. He flicked the piece of wood off. "Better?"

It was so not better. He had to be one of the handsomest men I had ever seen, and he wasn't shy at all. He could be quiet, but that wasn't the same thing as being shy. He always seemed to be taking everything in before he answered.

Luke stepped closer. I already knew what was coming before his lips met mine. This man was like a stick of dynamite and he didn't know it. Or maybe he did?

Luke flashed me a sexy grin as he picked up more wood and started chopping it. I couldn't stop myself from watching my husband work if I tried. Every move he made was deliberate and sure of himself. I helped Luke stack the wood again when he was finished chopping.

"Can I ask you something?" I readjusted the wood on the stack.

"Shore." Luke leaned on the wood pile glimmering.

"Do you like chopping wood?" I hated the chore, but I liked watching Luke do it.

Luke smiled at me curiously and nodded. "It's always been one of my favorites."

"Good." I was relieved.

"Let me guess." He stepped closer. "It's not one of your favorites?"

I shook my head no. The hairs on the back of my neck stood up. Flashes of last night ran through my mind. The better I got to know Luke, the more handsome he was. He was constantly doing things to make my life easier.

"Okay. It'll be mine from now on." My husband tucked a stray hair behind my ear and time stood still.

"Thank you." Everything about this man set me on edge and drew me closer to him.

"Anything else you need, Mrs. Larson?" His voice was low and husky.

I found my head shaking no. "I... uh, it's almost suppertime."

"Too bad." He smiled again before picking up his shirt and buttoning up as he headed back to the main house.

I couldn't figure Luke out. He never complained. He already had a chore done before it needed done. My sister never volunteered to do any outside chores. Pa had been doing the bare minimum for quite some time. It was nice to be around a man that cared as much as I did.

Luke

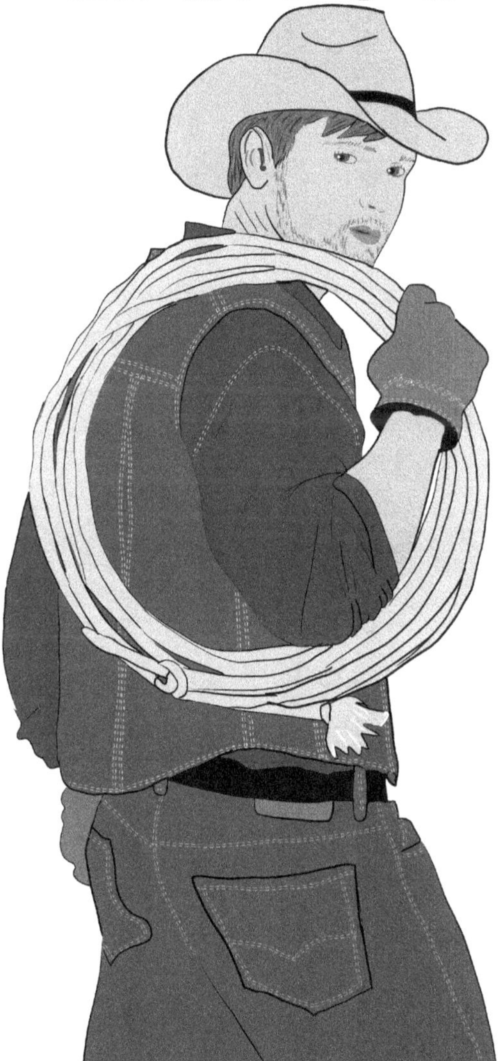

Sixteen
16

"Tommy, let's go." I didn't wait for my brother to answer.

Instead, I got on my horse and glanced over my shoulder. Tommy climbed up on the horse. He didn't have as much as experience as I have, but he was able to stay on the horse.

I started with a slow walk. Tommy kept my pace. Gradually, I sped up. I didn't stop until I was at the other end of the property.

Cold was setting in, but I wanted to get a start on the home I would share with Lucy. I was going to take advantage of every day I could until it was too cold to make the trip out here. I figured that meant I only had two or three weeks max to get some projects finished.

I got off the horse and tied my horse to a tree. Tommy came over and did the same. I checked the tie behind him. He had done it right. I removed two shovels from the saddle. I handed one to Tommy.

"What's this for?" Tommy frowned.

"We're digging a cellar." I walked over to the hill behind where I planned to build the house.

"Do you even know how to do that?" Tommy stared at the shovel like it was a foreign object.

"I got an idea." I growled.

Tommy wasn't far off. It'd been a while, but I remember Pa telling me how to build one. Once I heard how to do something, I was usually pretty good about figuring it out. We both started digging.

"I think we should eat soon." Tommy lifted the dirt out of the hole.

My stomach was tight as I thought about food. "Maybe so." I finally agreed.

I undid the flap on my saddle and pulled out some of the food Ma had prepared for us before we left. I didn't like that I was eating without Lucy, but this was an investment in our future.

"Are you shore you want to live all the way out here?" Tommy was doubtful.

"With Lucy. Yeah." I nodded, and I meant it. This was where our children would be born one day.

"You like her, huh?" Tommy grinned.

Like her, of course I liked her. Lucy was... my wife. Since day one, I felt responsible for her. More than that, I wanted to make her happy. The way she felt in my arms when we kissed... I didn't want to live one day without Lucy by my side.

"Your squirming brother." Tommy grinned.

"We have a lot of work to do." I got up and put the clothes that wrapped our food back in the saddlebag.

"Way to change the subject." Tommy laughed.

"Now that we know you can move your mouth, let's see you move the shovel." I challenged him.

"Shore thing, Luke." Tommy laughed again.

"With us working together, it shouldn't take too long." I picked up my shovel.

"Do you think Ma likes it here?" Tommy picked up his shovel. "It's a long way from her friends and Uncle Billy's family."

I stopped. "I think Ma would say something if she was unhappy."

"Maybe? Maybe not?" Tommy shrugged.

It occurred to me that he might not have meant Ma. I eyed my brother as he dug. He didn't say anything.

"What about you, Tommy? Are you happy here?" I kept digging.

"I miss my friends and I miss Pa, but it's okay here." Tommy shrugged. "Lucy's real nice and the foods good here."

Something still felt off. "Anything else?"

"I'd like my own room." Tommy glanced at me.

"If we get this house built soon, the building we're staying in will be empty or there is the barn loft come spring." I filled my shovel with dirt.

"Do you think Ma would let me sleep in the loft?" Tommy was excited.

"I think so." I emptied the shovel. "I'll talk to Lucy about it."

"Thanks, Luke." Tommy grinned.

Lucy

Seventeen
17

I watched my husband dismount from his horse. The mere sight of him made my heart race. Tommy followed Luke into the barn.

Luke had only been here for a week and he had stocked up the wood for the winter. He helped me feed the animals every morning. He had Tommy helping out mucking the stalls and helping with our house.

Tommy had moved into the barn loft. Luke and Tommy had repaired the fence in the south field that I had put off for the last month. It would have taken me half the winter to do all of that.

Everything about Luke drew me in. I passed the small one-room shack we shared. We needed a real bedroom. I felt myself blushing. The thought of sharing a real home with Luke was appealing for many reasons.

Tommy waved at me as he came running out of the barn, leaving Luke alone. I waved to my brother-in-law. I was glad Luke was alone in the barn. I had missed him.

As soon as Luke saw me enter the barn, he started grinning. I couldn't stop smiling as I headed straight for my husband. I think he might have missed me too.

"Hi." My heart picked up speed.

Luke sauntered over. "It took three days, but the cellar is done."

"You seem pretty determined." I took a step closer.

"I am, when I have a goal in mind." Luke's smile softened.

"Thank you." I whispered.

"For?" Luke cocked his eyebrow.

"Coming." I held his gaze.

Luke touched my cheek. "I missed you too."

"I didn't say that I missed you." I tried to keep my poker face in place.

Luke nodded twice and leaned forward to cover my lips with his. I wrapped my arms around him. He was solid. Something about this man turned up my temperature and made me want to be around him more.

Luke pulled back. "I'm glad I came too."

"What are you doing tomorrow?" I was curious.

"Did you need me for something?" Luke's voice was deeper.

I swallowed. I felt a fire poker to my soul. I was falling for my new husband.

"I have to go to town tomorrow for supplies. I thought you might..." I shifted my weight.

"I'd love to come, Sweetheart." Luke flashed me a smile. "Anywhere you want."

I felt warm from head to toe. "Well... I... well..."

Luke's smile grew.

"Yes... uh..." I fumbled.

"You're prettier than a sunset." Luke grinned.

"And you, Luke Larson, are a sweet talker." I put a hand on his chest.

Luke's eyes darkened. "It ain't sweet talking if it's the truth."

I laughed.

My husband smiled.

When we were together like this, it felt like our souls were touching. Words weren't necessary. The bond between us was growing as each day passed.

"Dinner should be ready." I swallowed.

"Probably." Luke put a hand on my cheek. "I'm still waiting for you to admit you missed me."

I bit my lower lip and shook my head.

Luke chuckled. "Come on, Sweetheart. I know you can say the words."

I laughed. "Maybe a little."

"Maybe a little what?" He leaned closer.

"Maybe I missed you." I was trying not to smile.

"Maybe?" Luke's eyebrows went up.

"Okay, I missed you. Can we go eat dinner now?" I took a step toward the barn door.

My husband laughed. "You know I missed you."

"I know." I paused in the doorway.

Luke's warm gaze made me think about the nights we spent alone. I tried to push down my emotions and failed. He made me think and feel things I never thought I would think about.

Luke made me want to be a good wife. He made me want to be a mother. He made me want to share the burden of this farm with him.

Growing up, I never wanted to share a life with any man. Now that Luke was in my life, I never wanted to live my life alone again. By the way he was smiling at me I didn't have to.

Luke

Eighteen
18

Lucy walked out of the main house toward me. It made Beth Ann mad that my wife refused to wear a dress. It didn't matter much to me. The pants hugged her hips as she made her way to the wagon and hopped up.

"Ready?" I let my gaze travel over her.

"I am." Lucy nodded.

I flicked the reins, and we started towards town.

"Do you have a blacksmith around here?" I glanced towards Lucy.

"We do. Why?" Lucy turned her attention toward me.

"I'm going to try to get started on the fireplace this week. I thought he might have some ideas." I wanted to do this right for Lucy.

"Already?" Lucy was surprised.

I nodded. "The cellar and outhouse are done. I think Tommy and I can gather the stones for the fireplace this week... if we can find enough stones, we'll build one."

"There is a pile of rocks by the garden." Lucy offered.

"Is it enough for a chimney?" I tried to think about how many rocks it would take to make a fireplace.

"If it's not, I'm sure someone has a rock pile in their backyard around here." Lucy's leg brushed mine.

"You're full of ideas." I smiled at my beautiful wife.

"So are you." Lucy blushed.

I loved being alone with Lucy. It made me sad to see the town coming into view. I parked the wagon.

"The blacksmith shop is down there." Lucy pointed.

"Okay. I'll meet you back here in half an hour?" I suggested.

Lucy nodded.

I watched my wife go inside of the General Store. We wouldn't be able to come into town nearly as much when it started snowing. On the next trip to town, we would need to make sure we were set for winter.

I made my way down the road to the blacksmith. He was pulling something out of the water with tongs. I waited until he put it down before I cleared my throat.

"What can I do for you, Mr." The man eyed me curiously.

"I'm Luke Larson." I stuck out my hand.

"Avery Turnbull." He shook my hand.

"Good to meet you. I'll get right to it. Lucy and I just got married. I was planning on building a house for us. I thought you might have some advice." I put my hands in my pocket.

"Sure do. When do you plan on building it?" Mr. Turnbull leaned on the back wall.

"Maybe before the next snowfall." I hoped I would be able to get our home started.

"Whew." Mr. Turnbull shook his head. "You're an ambitious one."

"Yes, sir. I have my brother helping me." I had about two weeks before snowfall. Maybe three weeks if I was lucky?

"Do you have money for the supplies?" Mr. Turnbull eyed me.

"Yes, sir." I had taken money out of the coffee can I shared with Ma and Tommy this morning.

"You're going to need..." Mr. Turnbull helped me load up with supplies from his shop and the General Store. He gave me some advice and headed back to his shop after I paid him.

I walked inside of the General Store. Lucy had two boxes sitting on the counter. I took one of the boxes out to the wagon and came back for the other. Lucy came outside.

I started to head back in.

"Did you need something?" Lucy was confused.

"I didn't pay for the supplies yet." I pointed to the wagon.

"I did." Lucy got in the wagon.

I climbed into the wagon with her. It occurred to me that I wasn't sure what the money situation was. It was high time I found out.

Lucy

Nineteen
19

Luke unloaded the last box out of the wagon. I liked watching his muscles flex. Having him here cut the unloading time in half.

"I'm heading out to the... our place... the..." Luke pointed.

"I got it." I laughed.

"Do you want to come with me?" Luke leaned on the wagon.

I glanced at the main house and then the barn. With Luke around, I wasn't nearly as behind for the day after going to town as I would have been doing this solo.

"Yeah." I opened the front door. "Luke and I will be back by suppertime."

"Have fun." Luke's Ma, Millie, smiled at me.

"I have to run to the outhouse first." It had been a while since I've been.

"Okay." Luke hopped in the wagon and waited.

I returned a few minutes later and hopped up in the wagon.

"We're going to try the wagon and see how far it gets." Luke made an adorable face.

"Well, you've been going out there every day, so there is a better chance the wagon will make it. Maybe if we go slow?" I suggested.

"I can do that." Luke flicked the reins, and the wagon moved forward.

The day was chilly, but the cold weather hadn't quite settled in yet. When snow hit out here, it tended to hit hard.

"Can I ask you something?" Luke seemed nervous.

"You're my husband, Luke. You can ask me anything. I might even have an answer." I flashed him a teasing smile.

"It occurred to me when I went to pay today, I didn't know... you know... what the money situation is?" Luke looked like he was ready to throw up, asking me the question.

"Oh." I swallowed.

"Is that okay to ask?" My husband had a pained expression.

"Yeah." I nodded.

"It's not that I'm money hungry or anything, but all I really have to contribute to this marriage is me." Luke shrugged.

"We have enough." I bit my lower lip. I wasn't used to talking about money.

"When you go to town, what do you normally do?" Luke's face was in a tight line.

"I usually take money out of the lock box and take it into town with me." I hadn't thought this through yet.

"Ma will want her own money." Luke stared ahead.

"What about you?" I was trying to figure out this marriage thing.

"I was raised that a man should provide for his family." His warm gaze landed on me.

"How about this? The extra money we earn from the extra fields you plan to work in the spring can go into your pocket. If your Ma is any good at making apple butter, we have a few apple trees behind the house. That way she can make money too." I suggested.

"Any money I earned from the field would be our money for our family." Luke slowed the wagon down to a slow walk.

"I know, but that way you won't feel like you're asking me for money." I put a hand on his leg.

My husband nodded his head twice as he mulled it over.

"Besides, we wouldn't be working that land without you, so Pa isn't expecting that income." I added.

"What will your Pa say?" Luke had a somber expression on his handsome face.

"Pa told me that he was leaving the farm to me and Beth Ann when he died, and I may as well start running it now." I smirked.

"Working the fields should make enough money to get Tommy some new shoes. That boy is growing faster than a weed." Luke chuckled.

I pulled a few bills out of my pocket. It should be enough for Luke to buy shoes and odds and ends until winter was over. I put it in Luke's hand.

Luke tried to hand it back.

"No, keep it. If you, Tommy, or your Ma need anything, I don't want you to feel like you have to ask me for the money. Besides, you've more than earned it with all of the work you've done on the farm so far." I handed it back to him.

"Okay." Luke put the money in his pocket.

I leaned into Luke, and he put his arm around me. My heart beat faster. I wanted Luke to be happy here.

"You're a good man, Luke Larson." I nuzzled closer to my husband.

"I'm glad you think so." Luke's warm breath hit my face.

"I know so." I smiled at him.

Luke had a soft chuckle on his lips as our home came into view. It hasn't been built yet, but it was there. I could see where the house was going to be.

The wagon came to a stop. The horses neighed. They were ready to get back to the warm barn.

"Welcome home." Luke grinned.

"You know, it already feels like home to me too." I couldn't keep the smile off my face.

Luke

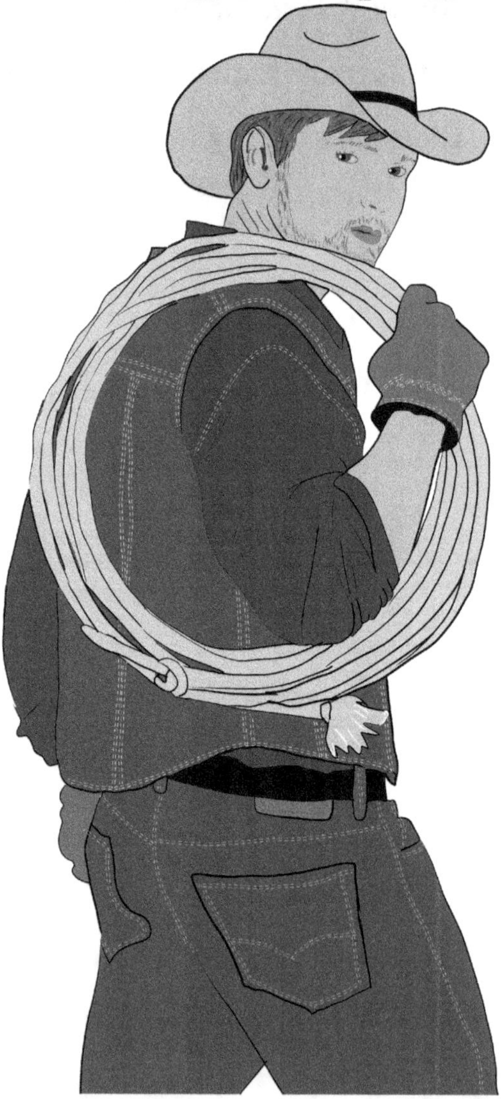

Twenty
20

By some miracle, the rain and snow had held off. Tommy and I put a pump in the yard. Mr. Turnbull suggested I build the house around the water pump. The same spring ran right through where I planned on putting the kitchen, so Tommy and I put a water pump in the kitchen too. Eventually, I planned on putting a barn out back.

Lucy's cousins, Russell and Frank, were coming over today to help frame the house. I have never met them before, but Lucy's Pa said they were good men. Tommy and Beth Ann were out of school. Tommy was pretty strong. I don't know what we would get finished up today.

"I see horses!" Tommy slammed the door behind him.

"Tommy, try not to slam the door." Ma rolled her eyes.

"Sorry, Ma." Tommy ran over to the counter and took a cookie out of the cookie jar when he didn't think anyone was looking.

I took a drink of my coffee and pretended that I didn't see him.

"Do you want me to come with you?" Lucy sat down with her full mug of coffee.

"No, you got work to do here." I shook my head.

It was my responsibility to build us a house, not Lucy's. Yes, I wanted her with me, but she did have work to do here. I had to do this for us.

"If you change your mind..." Lucy gave me a hard stare.

"I'll let you know." I promised.

Lucy nodded her head and took a drink of her coffee. The door flew open. Two men walked in, both were older than me. There were gray strands in their beards.

"Beth Ann, get over here and give me a hug." The man with a red tinted beard picked up Beth Ann and hugged her.

"Put me down, Frank!" Beth Ann giggled.

"Do you have any sweets around here? I know you have a sweet tooth." Frank laughed.

"You are the one with a sweet tooth." Beth Ann put her hand on her hip.

Frank scanned the kitchen. A large smile covered his face as he walked to the counter. He opened the cookie jar and had a handful of cookies out, before Beth Ann could close the lid.

"Frank!" Beth Ann stood between Frank and the cookie jar.

Frank put a cookie in his mouth.

"I'll take some of those, Beth Ann." The other man had a black beard.

"Now, I'm going to have to make more cookies!" Beth Ann turned around and pulled out several cookies and handed them to the second man.

The man with the black beard turned toward me. "Russell."

"Luke." I shook his extended hand.

"You ready to work?" Russell put a cookie in his mouth.

"Yes, sir." I stood up.

"Come on, Frank." Russell was the first out the door.

Tommy and I followed the two men outside. I wasn't sure what to expect, but I needed all the help I could get. I still needed two fireplaces, and the house built. With each day being colder than the last, I was running out of time.

"Have you built a house before?" Russell stopped beside of his horse.

"No, sir." I admitted.

"Don't worry, we know what we're doing." Russell put his foot in the stirrup and climbed on the horse.

"We've built a few barns too." Frank put a cookie in his mouth and ate it.

"Luke wants to put a barn out there." Tommy climbed into the wagon full of lumber.

"We'll see what we can do." Russell nodded.

"Thanks for coming." I nodded.

"That's what family's for." Russell tipped his hat.

I got in the wagon with Tommy, and we led the way out to my place. When the outhouse came into view, happiness hit me. I knew it was silly, but this place was my home, even without the building.

Russell and Frank got off of their horses and tied them to the tree.

"I see you have bricks and stone for the fireplace." Russell approached the area with the supplies.

"You have two water pumps." Frank pointed to the one in the middle of the yard and the one closer to the fireplace.

"Mr. Turnbull suggested it. Sounded like a good idea." I put my hands around my suspenders.

"I like it." Frank nodded.

"Tell us what you have planned." Russell put his elbow on his brother's shoulder.

"I was thinking we could build a main room here with a fireplace and a bedroom here. I'd like to add another bedroom there." I pointed to the side of the house.

"He wants two fireplaces." Tommy confided.

"Frank is the expert when it comes to chimneys and fireplaces." Russell stood straight and nodded towards his brother.

"The best in the county." Frank grinned.

"Tommy, why don't you give Frank a hand and Luke and I will start on the house?" Russell gave the orders.

Russell seemed to know what he was doing. We worked until it was time for the midday meal. Tommy and Frank had one of the fireplaces chest high. It would have taken me at least a week if not longer. I wasn't sure what I was doing, so I would have been guessing, but it looked like a real fireplace.

Russell and I had built the floor to the bedroom, so we stayed out of Frank and Tommy's way. We left space for him to add a fireplace in there too. We had gotten a lot done in a few hours.

"Frank and I will come by tomorrow." Russell's gaze met mine.

I nodded.

Russell flicked his reins and his horse bolted off. Frank passed us in the empty wagon. I took one last look.

"Frank's a hoot." Tommy laughed.

"Did you learn anything?" I flicked the reins and headed back to Lucy.

"I learned a lot. Frank said if I ever need a job, I can help him out." Tommy grinned.

I messed up my brother's hair.

"Luke!" Tommy fixed his hair.

I chuckled.

"I'm glad they're coming back tomorrow. It will make the work easier." Tommy leaned forward.

"It sure will. Thanks, Tommy. You've been a big help." I don't know how I would have gotten this far without him.

"That's what family's for, right Luke?" Tommy smiled at me.

"That's right." I grinned.

Lucy

Twenty-One
21

Luke had been really quiet this week. He left early in the morning and was returning in time for supper. I know he was working on our house, but I didn't see how he would finish it before snowfall, even with Russell and Frank helping out all last week.

I was concerned about winter. There was already a morning chill in the air when we woke up. We had plenty of extra quilts stored in the loft of the main house. I hoped it was enough to keep us all warm through the winter. I was probably fretting over nothing.

Luke was warmer than the warm brick that Ma used to wrap up for me and Beth Ann at night. This was the first year that I wasn't under the same roof as Pa and Beth Ann. We had plenty of blankets and a brick to keep us warm if we really needed it.

The room Luke and I were sharing didn't have any heat and it would take more than a brick to keep us warm when the temperatures dropped below freezing. It hadn't been a problem so far. Luke was always warm. As long as he was beside me, I doubt the cold would bother me much.

We'd been married less than a month and Luke had already made a lot of changes on the farm. All of them were good so far. Waking up with Luke to do chores was one of the best parts of my day.

Luke had his mind set on building us a home. I knew we needed one. The problem was that I was missing him more than I thought I would.

Luke had a calm spirit and a gentle soul. He had a firm sense of right and wrong that came out in any conversation that lasted more than a minute. He was a hard-working, attractive man.

I kept glancing down the pathway that would lead to my home with Luke. It was time for my husband to come back to me. Something moved in the distance. It was only a rabbit.

I leaned on the fence post. I couldn't get any-thing done at this time of day, because I kept seeing if he was coming home. I heard the faint sound of horse hooves in the distance. We didn't have any close neighbors.

I shielded my eyes and watched until Luke and Tommy came galloping my way. I couldn't help smiling as Luke and Tommy raced toward the barn.

I felt pleasure and a mixture of pride rush through me as Luke won. Luke said something to Tommy that I couldn't hear. Tommy wasn't happy about it. I laughed to myself as I walked toward the barn.

Tommy was taking care of his horse as I arrived. He put his horse in the stall. I had already put food and water out for both horses.

"Hi, Lucy!" Tommy waved.

"Hi, Tommy." I waved back.

Tommy took off running out of the barn.

A slow grin appeared on Luke's handsome lips when I stepped closer.

"I missed you." I felt like a candle turned on in my soul when he smiled at me like that.

"I missed you too." Luke leaned down and kissed me.

"Did you have a good day?" I didn't budge from his embrace.

"It was okay. We got a lot of work done. I have a few things I want to finish up, before you see it." Luke had a twinkle in his eyes.

"You know I hate waiting." I made a face.

"Trust me, it will be work the wait." Luke's smile reached his eyes.

"Luke, hurry up! Ma says supper is ready!" Tommy yelled from the front porch of the main house.

"We're coming!" Luke hollered back.

Luke

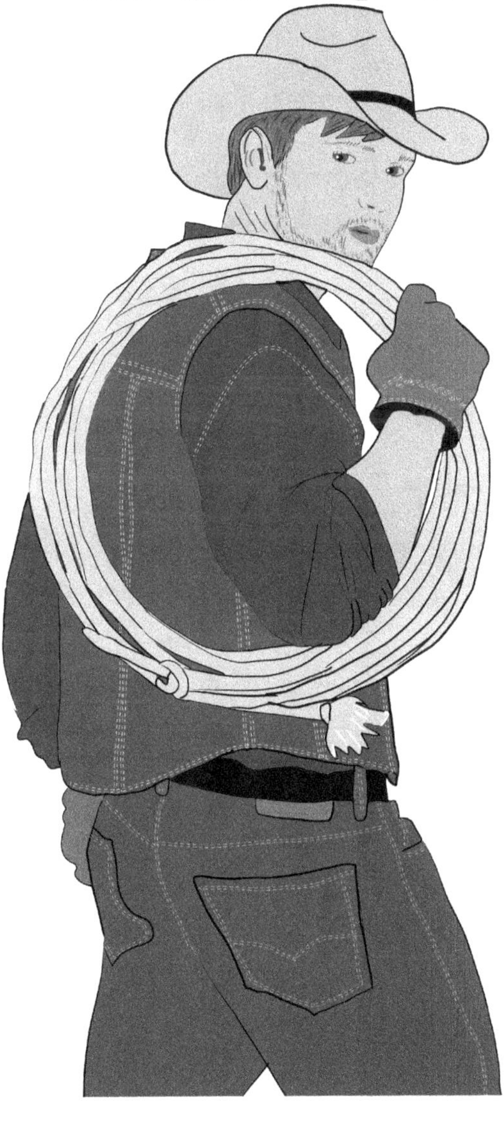

Twenty-Two
22

I moved the plane along the edge of the wood. A few more strokes later, I put the plane aside and touched the wood. It was somewhat smooth.

I picked up the plane again and ran it along the edge of the wood. A few minutes later, I put the plane aside and ran my fingers over the door. I deemed it done. I unscrewed the clamps and leaned the door up against the wall.

Pa had taught me how to make stuff out of wood as soon as I could walk. I'd missed working with wood like this when I lived with Uncle Billy. It was nice to get back to my roots.

I picked up the door hinge and marked the end of the door around the door hinge. I took the plane off and put the second on the bottom of the door, and marked the outline of the hinge. I proceeded to chisel out the depth of the door hinge. I smoothed it out with my finger. It was flat enough.

I haven't done this kind of work without my Pa around. I could feel him walking around me, checking every move I made. I closed my eyes for a moment, so tears wouldn't escape. Working with wood gave me plenty of time to think, but sometimes I got lost in the wrong thoughts.

I put the hinge in the hole at the top of the door and ran my finger around the edge of the wood to the metal. The metal in the far corner wasn't flush. I removed the hinge and chiseled the corner. I ran my finger over the wood. It looked like it would work.

I put the hinge on the wood. I ran my finger around the edge of the wood and metal. I was satisfied.

Pride filled my house. My Pa wasn't shy about praise when Tommy or I did a good job. He would have bragged to Ma before I got a chance to show her my work. I smiled at the memories. Thinking about him now, made me feel like he was still here.

I leaned the door against the wall and walked with the hinge of my hand and dug through my tools to find a screwdriver. My hand landed on it. I grabbed a few screws and walked back over. I readjusted the door and started screwing in the screw. It wasn't working. I groaned.

I put everything down and walked over to my tools and located a nail. I grabbed the hammer and put a few practice holes in the door where the hinge should go. I did it on the bottom of the door too.

I put the hammer down and slid the nail into my pocket. I took the screwdriver and screw and started screwing in the hinges. I was finally done.

"Tommy! Get in here!" I yelled.

The steady sound of the ax stopped. I took a drink. I heard a steady thump of wood falling onto a pile. Tommy walked in and took the cup from my hand and took a drink.

"You finally finished?" Tommy put the cup down.

"Shut up and help me." I put a small piece of wood on the floor about six inches from the door hinge.

I picked up the door and put it on the wood. "Tommy." I gestured for him to hold the door.

Tommy took hold of it. "Got it."

I moved the door until it was where I needed it to be. The door moved two inches to the left. "Tommy, hold it steady." I growled.

"I am." Tommy held it straight.

I marked the outline of the hinge at the top of the door. Tommy and I put it against the wall. I chiseled it out. I repeated the process with the nail and hammer.

"Help me." I gestured toward the door. We picked it up. The door fit perfectly in the door hinge. "Hold it steady." I ordered.

I marked out the bottom of the door hinge. We moved it against the wall again. I chiseled out the bottom hinge. I used the nail and hammer to put in a few holes in the bottom hinge.

"Tom. Now." I walked over to the door.

Tommy grabbed the door with me, and we put it back on the wood. I moved it around and started screwing the hinge at the top of the door. I left some wiggle room. I bent down and moved the door, so the hinge lined up. I began to screw in the door. I left a little wiggle room at the bottom.

I stood up and pushed the wood out of the way. Tommy took a step back. I moved the door back and forth. I tightened it on the top and moved it. It worked. I finished tightening the bottom.

"You good now?" Tommy raised his eyebrows.

"Yeah." I grumbled.

I located the strike plate. I put it against the wood and marked out where it was going to go. I started chiseling out the spot. A few minutes later, I was able to close the door. I moved it back and forth three times. It seemed fine. There was a knock on the door. I opened it.

"Are we done for today?" Tommy huffed.

"Yeah." I nodded and closed the door behind me.

I couldn't wait to show Lucy. I prayed she loved it as much as I did. Getting on my horse, I felt lighter. We had managed to finish before the first snowfall.

"Does this mean I can move into your room?" Tommy grinned.

I chuckled. "I reckon so."

"Is it okay if I stay in the barn? I've kind of gotten used to the animal noises at night." Tommy shrugged.

I laughed. "I don't think Ma will mind as long as you're warm."

"Are you sure you and Lucy will be okay out here?" Tommy turned to look at my home.

"Lucy and I will be just fine." Of that, I was sure.

Lucy

Twenty-Three
23

"**A**re you ready to see the house?" Luke was excited.

"Are you ready to show me?" I teased.

Luke had been secretive about the house since he started building it. He refused to let me come help him. He said he wanted it to be a surprise. He had been working on it for three weeks.

I knew Russell and Frank came out for a week and worked on it. Tommy was out there every time Luke went out. I was trying to imagine how much work they could get done in that amount of time, but I wasn't sure.

"Let's go." I grinned.

"The horses are ready to go." Luke was practically bouncing.

"Look at you, thinking of everything." I kissed my husband's cheek.

"I try." Luke put his hand on my back and led me to the barn.

The horses flew to the house that Luke built for us like they knew the way home. The path between the barn and our new home was beaten down from all of the trips Luke made out there with Tommy and my cousins.

I'd been curious, but I decided to stay away until Luke wanted to show me. My mouth fell open as the house came into view. There was an outhouse and a house with a roof. I could see two chimneys on either side of the house. It was fancier than I was expecting.

Luke slid off his horse and tied it to a tree near the house. I did the same. I couldn't believe he did this for us. Pride flooded through me for my husband. This was his vision come to life. I would never have built a house out here on my own.

"What do you think?" Luke whispered.

"I want to see the inside." I smiled at my husband.

Luke crossed the yard and opened the door. It was dark inside of the main room, but a kerosene lantern would fix that. The fireplace was begging to heat the chilly room.

I touched the walls as I walked to the fireplace. There was a mantle with matches sitting on it. Inside of the fireplace were burned ashes. Luke, Tommy, and my cousins had done an amazing job in a short amount of time.

I walked over to the counter. A water pump was in the house! I was impressed. Most houses around here didn't have running water.

"I didn't know you were so talented." I took a step closer to him.

"So you like it?" His warm voice was soft.

I nodded my head.

"I don't think I could have done it without Russell and Frank. I'd still be working on the fireplace. Tommy was a big help too." Luke was glowing.

"Thank you." I touched his forearm.

Luke stepped closer. "I'm invested in our future."

I glanced around. "I'm starting to see that."

"We need to send for windows and a stove." Luke's eyes sparkled with excitement. "We can add a room through there." He pointed.

My eyes turned to the wall behind us. He had thought this through. I didn't think he would actually finish this house before the first snowfall. He proved me wrong. When Luke Larson made up his mind, I had a feeling nothing could stop him.

"So...?" Luke wrapped his large arms around me and pulled me against his chest.

I felt warmth cover my cheeks immediately.

"Do you think you could be happy here?" Luke's deep voice whispered in my ear.

"I think I could be happy anywhere you are." It was the truth.

"Really?" Luke's heart was on his sleeve.

"Really." I wrapped my arms around his neck and we shared a sweet kiss.

Luke

Twenty-Four
24

Now that the house was built, I wanted to fill it with furniture. Dad had taught me how to work with wood, but Mr. Gregor was the one that brought my skills to the next level.

I spent one summer helping out Mr. Gregor. He lived down the street, making cabinets for his kitchen. It was a lot of detail work. I wanted that for Lucy. My wife deserved the best that I could give her. With winter practically here, it might have to turn into a winter project.

I'd always wanted the kind of workshop Mr. Gregor had. When we lived with Uncle Billy, we had to sell Pa's tools to make ends meet. I wish I still had some of his tools, but all I had left was Pa's pocket knife.

If we built a barn behind our home, I might be able to turn part of it into a workshop. Mr. Gregor had a side business with his skills. Maybe I could too?

We still had lumber around from the house, but we'd need some more to build a barn. If I could get a few men to help me, the barn would go up pretty quickly. I've been to a few barn raisings in my time. I had to go talk to my wife, and see what she thought about it.

"Lucy." I found her in the barn brushing down her horse.

She stopped and turned toward me.

"I had an idea." My hands started getting sweaty. I rubbed them on my pants.

"An idea?" Lucy's beautiful blue eyes narrowed.

"Would it be out of line to have a barn raising for our new home?" I found my hands awkward, so I shoved them in my pockets. I didn't like asking for help, but I didn't have the luxury of time.

Lucy brushed the horse a few more times, before putting the horse back in the stall. I wasn't sure what she thought of the idea. I really wanted this for us.

"Do we really need two barns on the property?" She stepped closer.

"We need a place for the horses by our place." I pointed. "Especially in the winter."

Lucy nodded.

"I was thinking about opening a woodworking business. I could turn half of the barn into a workshop." I met her gaze.

"Really?" Lucy was surprised.

I nodded. "I'm good with my hands."

Lucy blushed slightly. "Okay. We can ask after church."

I kissed Lucy on her cheek.

She grinned at me.

"What?" I wasn't sure what that smile meant.

"You sure are something special, Luke." Lucy's gaze had had something in her eyes that wasn't there before.

"Do you think there is a market around here for furniture and cabinets?" I hadn't met everyone in the community, so I didn't know if someone already did something like that around here.

"I do." Lucy leaned on the beam in the middle of the barn.

"I'd still help out around the farm, but it would give me something to do during the winter." I started dreaming up projects to make.

"You really want this, don't you?" Lucy examined me.

"I do." I nodded my head.

"Luke, you've already done so much for me and my family. If having a workshop would make you happy, I think you should have it." Lucy's blue eyes had me enamored with her.

I stepped closer to her. "Lucy, I'd do anything for you."

"There you go, sweet-talking me again, Luke Larson." Lucy flashed me a teasing smile.

I chuckled.

"It's working." Lucy wrapped her arms around my neck.

Standing in the barn holding each other had quickly become one of my favorite spots. I bent down and placed a kiss on her lips. Kissing Lucy ignited a fire every time I touched her.

"I love you, Lucy." I didn't mean for the words to come out, but it was true.

Lucy's smile faltered for a second. It was enough time to send me into a full-blown panic attack. I should have kept my mouth shut, but the words slipped out.

"I love you too, Luke." Lucy's smile was shy.

"Really?" I bit my lower lip.

Lucy nodded her beautiful head.

I picked Lucy up and spun her in a circle. Lucy saying that she loved me was the best feeling in my entire life. I couldn't imagine anything better.

"Can you say that again?" I whispered as I put her down.

"I love you." Lucy giggled.

"I love you too." I couldn't wipe the grin off of my face if I tried.

Lucy wrapped her arms around my waist and laid her head on my chest. I leaned my chin on her head. The woman I was holding was next to perfection. I

couldn't have dreamed up any woman nearly as perfect for me as Lucy was. I kissed her forehead.

145

Lucy

Twenty-Five
25

The yard started to fill up with wagons. Beth Ann stood by the barn and pointed down the trail. It would be easier if we had a sign, but Beth Ann loved a good jawing session.

All of my chores at home were done. I couldn't wait to see the barn. Luke had been at it with the other men for a few hours. I couldn't wait any longer.

I walked into the main house and closed the door. Luke's Ma had a big pot of chili sitting on the stove. I poured myself a mug of coffee and took a drink.

"That smells amazing." I smiled at Luke's Ma.

"I figured the men would be hungry soon." She sat down at the table.

"Do you want me to ride out and tell them?" I was anxious to see how things were going.

"You don't have to. Luke said they would be here for the midday meal." Millie smiled.

"Oh." I was disappointed.

It was already almost midday. By the time I rode out there, they'd be heading our way. Millie patted the spot next to her, so I sat down.

"How is everything going with my son?" Millie passed the plate of cookies toward me.

"You raised a good man." I tried to keep my heart from racing.

Luke had a way of making every problem in my life not seem like a problem. If it was cold, that was a chance to chop wood or cuddle. We didn't have a house; that was an opportunity to build one.

"I'd like to think so." Millie chuckled.

Beth Ann ran through the door and closed it. "Millie makes the best cookies."

Beth Ann loaded up a plate and sat down next to me.

"I'm glad you like them. They're my Ma's recipe that she got from her Ma." Millie took a drink of her mug.

"I heard horses heading this way, so I thought I better get some before the men eat them all." Beth Ann demolished the second cookie.

"Why didn't you say so, child?" Millie got up and started loading chili into bowls.

The door flew open and Frank walked in.

"Why am I not surprised you are here first?" Beth Ann put a hand on her hip.

Frank chuckled. "I just wanted to make sure all of the cookies weren't gone." He loaded up his hand and started eating.

"You better save some for everyone else." Beth Ann shook her finger at him.

Frank chuckled and ate the next cookie. Beth Ann shook her head. I stood up.

"Lucy." Frank came over and gave me a big hug.

"Thanks for coming, Frank." I squeezed my cousin.

"Nothing you wouldn't have done for me." Frank let go of me and took a bowl of chili off the counter.

Beth Ann pulled out a spoon and put it in his bowl.

"Thank you." Frank took the spoon.

The door flew open, and more men came in. I started filling mugs with coffee. Beth Ann handed out the bowls. When the bowls were all being used, we started using plates and the smaller pots.

Beth Ann was starting in on the dishes when Luke walked in the door. I handed him my mug, since all of the other cups were being used. He took it from me and took a drink.

"How far along did you get?" I whispered.

"It's up." Luke smiled.

"Really?" I was surprised.

"There is still some work to do on the inside, but it's up and two stalls are already set up for our horses." Luke handed me his mug.

"Kitchen coop is done too." Russell winked at me.

"Thank you, Russell." I was surprised.

Beth Ann handed Luke a bowl of chili.

"Thank you." Luke took the bowl.

It didn't take long for the men to clear out of the house. Before I knew it, Luke and I were standing on the porch alone, watching the last horse leave.

"The house is ready." Luke eyed me.

I knew what he was really saying. He was wanting to know when we were going to move in. Dark clouds hovered in the sky. We were in for snow soon. If we moved in before the snowfall, we might be stuck out there by ourselves. It was decision time.

"Do you want to move in tonight?" I was anxious to see the barn, and I honestly didn't mind getting snowed in with Luke if it came to it.

A slow grin covered my husband's face. He crossed the porch, picked me up, and spun me around. I couldn't help laughing. Luke opened the door and poked his head in.

"Tommy, come give us a hand!" Luke hollered.

"Coming." Tommy called from inside of the main house.

Luke

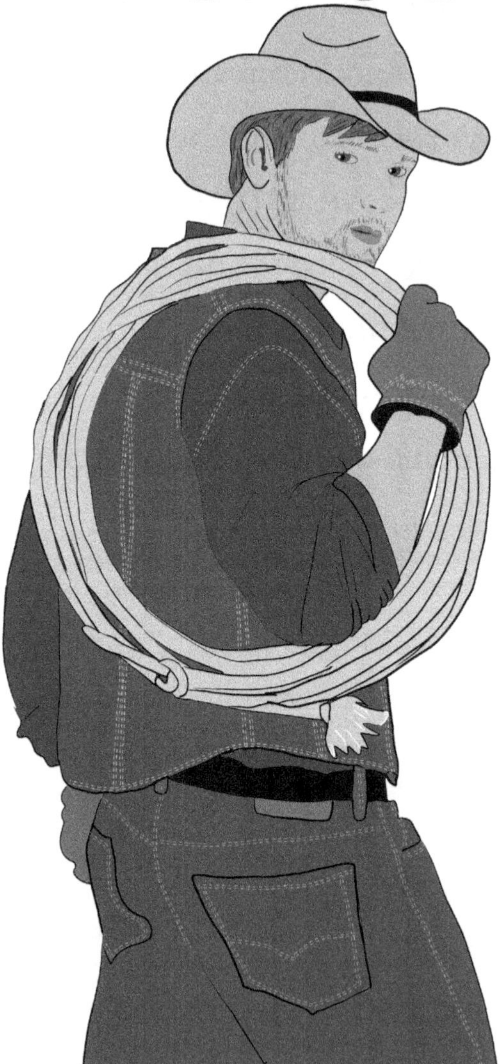

Twenty-Six
26

"That's all of it." Tommy grinned.

"Thank you." I messed up my brother's hair.

"Luke!" Tommy fixed his hair.

"Come on, I'll help you get the extra mat from out of the barn." I pointed to the barn.

"I got it, Luke." Tommy ran off.

"Horse feed." Lucy pointed at the back of the wagon.

"We'll bring out chickens and a rooster tomorrow." I put my arm around my wife's shoulders.

"If we can get back." Lucy chuckled.

"We'll get back." I nodded my head.

"If'in you say so." Lucy shrugged.

"Let's get home." I smiled.

"That has a nice ring to it." Lucy grinned at me and climbed into the wagon.

I climbed in beside her and flicked the reins. My body was aching from all of the hard work I've done today, but I felt good about what I accomplished.

"Are you happy you came, Luke?" Lucy leaned closer to me.

"Very happy." I kissed her temple.

I couldn't wait to see what Lucy thought of the barn. I wanted her to like it. I may not have been able to give her everything, but it was nice to know that I could give her a home.

"Almost there." I couldn't wipe the grin off of my face.

We rounded the bend, and the barn came into view. It was magnificent. I turned to my wife. I wanted to see her expression when she first saw it. Lucy's face lit up.

"Do you like it?" My heart was beating out of my chest.

Lucy nodded her head.

"If you want to change anything or you have any ideas, I'll do my best to make it happen." My words rushed out.

A tear escaped Lucy's eye and ran down her cheek.

"Are you okay?" A ton of bricks hit me in the gut.

Lucy bobbed her head yes.

"Then what's wrong? I didn't mean to make you cry." I swallowed.

"No one has gone to all of this trouble for me." Lucy's beautiful blue eyes were glistening when she looked at me.

"I'd do anything for you, Sweetheart." I put my hand on her leg.

Lucy wrapped her arm around my arm and put her head on my shoulder until the wagon came to a stop outside of the house. Lucy and I got out of the wagon. The two of us unloaded the wagon. The hardest part was getting the mattress into our bedroom, so we got that out of the way first. Then we tackled our clothes and other supplies.

"That's the last trunk." I pushed the trunk into our house and closed the door.

"I'll get the horses." Lucy placed a kiss on my cheek and walked out the door.

I scanned the room. This was it. I walked around my home proudly. I had built it, and now I was living here with my wife. Everything had changed a lot in the last few weeks; good changes. I couldn't have done it without Tommy or Lucy's cousins.

I unbuttoned my first couple of buttons on my coat. It was cold. Lucy would need to be warm.

I walked into the bedroom first. I let out a deep breath. It was just as cold in here. That needed to change.

I stared at the bed on the floor. I would need to build a bed frame soon, but the house was built. I could spend the winter working on furniture for the place.

First thing firs, we needed the house warmed up. I walked over to the fireplace and prepared a fire. Wind whistled down the chimney. I grabbed the box of matches off of the top of the mantelpiece and lit the fire. It took a few matches for it to catch, but I felt the heat immediately.

Time to take care of the Main room. I poked at the ashes in the fireplace of the main room. They collapsed. I started putting in more wood and stacking it. The flames took a few tries to catch, but the dancing flames lit up the room when they finally did.

I stood up. I put my hands over the fire. The warmth on my fingertips was instantaneous.

The door opened, and Lucy walked inside. She closed the door behind her. I stood up and turned around.

"Welcome home, Mrs. Larson." I made my way over to Lucy.

"Welcome home, Mr. Larson." She was walking towards me with a smile on her face.

"I love you." I wrapped my arms around her.

"I know you do." Lucy giggled.

I chuckled.

"I think we're going to be happy here." Lucy let me go.

"Me too." Warmth wasn't the only thing filling our home.

This was the first time either of us had really been on our own. The excitement in the air was tangible. Lucy walked to the bedroom and stopped in the door-way.

"What do you think?" I wrapped my arms around her from behind.

"It's perfect, Luke." Lucy turned around, and we shared a soul-warming kiss.

Lucy

Twenty-Seven
27

Our first Christmas was coming up. Since Ma died, we hadn't gone all out. It felt important to try harder this year. Tommy was a little younger than Beth Ann. This was still a magical time of year for him. That, and I wanted Luke and my first Christmas together to be rememberable.

I wasn't sure what to do. I would need a present for Luke. I let out a deep breath. What would he like? He was busy at the house. I took the opportunity to run into town without him knowing.

I found myself walking through the few aisles. I saw the thread. I picked it up. If I were more handy, I could make him something. I cringed. Although, I knew how to sew; I hated it worse than cooking.

It was unfair to ask Luke to come out here for me to be my husband. I wasn't good at being a wife.

Self-loathing captured me. I knew how to run the prop-erty, but a home? I didn't have the first clue... I froze. On the back shelf was a new set of tools.

"Can I look at those?" I pointed.

"Sure." Mr. Montgomery got them down.

I touched the chisels and other unfamiliar tools. I knew he had some, but... it was Christmas. Luke would love them, or at least I hoped he would.

"Do you have a sharpening set?" I scanned the wall.

"I think I have one in the back." Mr. Montgomery walked away and put the sharpening set on the counter a minute later. "What are you working on?"

"Not me, Luke." I smiled softly. "Christmas... if you can keep a secret."

Mr. Montgomery smiled. "I'll wrap them up for you."

"I'm going to pick out a few more things." I walked away from the counter.

"Take your time." Mr. Montgomery was already wrapping up the items.

I couldn't take too much time or Luke would notice I left the farm without telling him. I didn't want him to have any reason to ask me questions or it would ruin the surprise.

I found some fabric for Beth Ann. I picked out some candy for Tommy. I found a mystery book for Pa. I picked out some sewing supplies for Millie. I put the items on the counter.

"Is that all?" Mr. Montgomery started wrapping up the items.

I nodded.

Mr. Montgomery told me the price.

"Thank you for all of your help." I pulled the bills out of my pocket and put them on the counter.

Mr. Montgomery counted out my change and pushed the packages toward me in brown wrapped paper.

"Have a good day, Mrs. Larson." Mr. Montgomery smiled.

"Thank you." I smiled.

I walked out and slid the packages into my saddlebag. I felt relieved. I may not be the wife Luke deserved, but I knew I was better with him in my life and I wanted to make him happy. Before he came into my life, I had been consumed with work. Now, I really wanted the life we were building together.

I managed to hide the package and put away my horse before Luke came into the barn and put his horse in the stall. We have been eating our meals at the main house with our family and riding back home at night.

"Ready for dinner?" Luke smiled.

"Yeah." I swallowed. I hoped he didn't notice how nervous I was.

"What did you do today?" Luke leaned in and placed a soft kiss on my lips.

I shrugged. I needed to get out of this question quick. We haven't kept secrets from each other, and I wanted his Christmas present to be a surprise.

"I'm hungry." I spouted off before he could notice the change in me.

Luke extended an outstretched hand to me. I took it and we walked to the house hand in hand. My husband flashed me a smile as he opened the door. I was reminded again of just how sweet he was.

"Thank you." I whispered as I walked past him.

"Anytime, Sweetheart." His voice was low and warm.

The warm air hit me when I walked in. Millie had the table set when we walked in. I was happy to be here, but the place I grew up in no longer felt like home. The house Luke built was home now.

"We need to start planning for Christmas!" Beth Ann gushed.

"Are we going to get a tree?" Tommy joined in.

"Of course, we're going to get a tree." Beth Ann patted his hand.

"Do you have ornaments?" Millie put a plate on the table.

"We have some red paint. Maybe we could paint pinecones?" Beth Ann suggested.

"I love to paint." Tommy grinned.

"Then it's settled. We'll make ornaments tomorrow and Luke will cut down a tree." Millie smiled at my husband.

"I guess I'm cutting down a tree tomorrow." Luke chuckled.

"Make that two." I held up two fingers.

"You got it, Sweetheart." Luke's warm smile reached his eyes.

Luke

Twenty-Eight
28

Christmas was almost here. I needed to come up with something for Lucy; I just wasn't sure what.

We needed the house, so I didn't consider that a present. It was for both of us. I needed to come up with something else. What would Lucy want?

Lucy was a practical woman. She would want something she could use. I rubbed my jawline. This would take some thinking.

I got off my horse and tied it to the fence post. I noticed the fence was broken earlier this morning on my way to feed the animals. I took the shovel off of my saddle and dug a deeper hole. I pulled up the collapsed post and reset it. I carefully put dirt around it and nailed the wiring back in place.

My hands were busy, but my mind was searching for the perfect gift for my wife. I bit my lip. What could

I make her? I didn't have much money. I needed to get something for Ma and Tommy too.

I tested the fence. It held. I nodded my approval and slid my hammer back into my saddlebag. I picked up the shovel and attached it to the saddlebag.

I opted to go to town. I had to get something for them before all the good presents were gone.

I stopped by the barn. Lucy wasn't around. I frowned. I was about to leave when I heard a sound up in the loft.

"Lucy? Are you up there?" I called.

There was a floor creaking and the sound of boards being moved. I walked over to the ladder. Before I could climb up, Lucy poked her head over the side.

"Luke!" Lucy's hat fell to the floor.

I caught her hat midair. Lucy started climbing down the ladder. I took a step back and waited for her to climb down. I put the hat back on her head. I stepped closer and put my hands on her hips.

"What were you...?"

Lucy stood on her tiptoes and kissed me. I was surprised. I moved closer. The cold air disappeared around me. Lucy was like a flame when I touched her. I couldn't help smiling.

"Did you get the fence fixed?" Lucy whispered.

"I did." I didn't let her go.

"Any other plans for today?" Lucy grinned.

"This." I gave her one more kiss.

"I like those kinds of plans." Lucy nodded once.

"I was going into town to pick something up for Tommy for Christmas." I started tripping over my words.

"Okay." Lucy's eyes were curious. "You better hurry then." She gave me a light shove. "It'll be dark soon."

I didn't budge. I took her hand in mine and kissed her on the cheek before letting her hand go and getting back on my horse. I was warm from Lucy's kiss all the way to town.

I tied up my horse and headed into the General Store. Nothing jumped out at me for Lucy. Tommy would like almost everything in this store.

I finally decided on some thick rubber bands for Tommy; he'd been wanting to make his own sling shot.

I found some fabric that I thought Ma and Beth Ann might like. I picked out some shaving supplies for Lucy's Pa.

I put the items on the counter.

"Anything I can help you with?" Mr. Montgomery leaned on the counter.

"Just getting some Christmas presents for the family." I patted the counter.

"I'll get these wrapped up for you." Mr. Montgomery got out the brown paper.

Now, what was I going to get for Lucy?

"Do you have any ideas what my wife might like for Christmas?" I leaned over the counter.

Mr. Montgomery chuckled.

Lucy

Twenty-Nine
29

Keeping this secret from Luke was harder than I could imagine. I tucked Luke's present inside of my saddlebag. I only had to keep it a secret for 24 more hours.

I made my way back home over the cold grass. The sky was clouded. The chill was permanently in the air. I enjoyed the warm weather more, but staying cooped up with Luke for the winter had its perks.

I couldn't help smiling as I approached home. Home. Luke had done an amazing job with our home. He was planning to make a wrap-around porch in the spring after he added an extra bedroom or two.

I led my horse into the barn. All I could think about was the contents of my saddlebag. Luke had been looking at me suspiciously ever since I came back from town the other day. Did he already know about the present? It was hard to tell. I couldn't exactly ask him.

Luke had a blanket covering the area he was using as a workshop. It probably helped to keep the warm air in. It was a good idea.

My husband had a lot of good ideas. They weren't ideas that I would have thought up, like this place. If it were me, I might have added a room to the building we were living in, but honestly, I probably wouldn't have done that either. I had a way of getting stuck in a rut and doing the chores in the morning and fixing the things that went wrong during the day.

Luke was a dreamer. He wanted better for me than I wanted for myself. It was easier to just let him go and see what happened when he came back.

When I advertised for a husband, I didn't expect to fall in love with the man that came. I didn't expect him to be so kind or handsome either. I was lucky to have Luke in my life, and I knew it.

I put my horse away and put my saddle outside of the stall. Luke didn't use my saddle, so it should be safe in there until I can think of a better hiding place.

The house was pretty sparse. It might be best to keep it in the barn, there were more places to hide it.

"Lucy, is that you?" My husband came from behind the blanket.

I made a face at the saddlebag. Of course, he was in his workshop. Come on, Lucy, don't look at your saddlebag and he won't figure it out. It was a good thing Christmas was only a few days away. There was no way I could keep this secret much longer.

"Yeah, it's me Luke!" I called.

There was a clambering of tools being sat down. A second later, the blanket opened, and he came out. My husband had a smile on his face as he made his way over to me.

"Did you want to finish making ornaments for the tree?" Luke wrapped his arms around me.

I nodded my head.

"Let's get you inside and warm." Luke rubbed my back.

"That sounds good." I glanced at my saddlebag as we left the barn.

"Ma sent some lace with me earlier. She thought it might look pretty on the tree." Luke closed the barn door behind us.

"I like that idea." We walked inside to our warm house.

I've never lived in a house with two chimneys. It was luxurious to have a home this warm. The tree was sitting in the corner of our home. The ornaments that we made at the main house yesterday were sitting under the tree. I felt like a little girl again as I took off my coat and began decorating it with Luke.

Luke

Thirty
30

I woke up with Lucy in my arms. I pulled her closer. Some would call our life together luck. I would call it God, knowing I needed her in my life. She could have easily told me no; she changed her mind when I showed up, but she didn't. Not everyone would be okay with me dragging my brother and Ma with me to a place I didn't know, but it had worked out.

A lot had changed about my life since Pa died. I glanced at my wife. Would he have liked Lucy? I don't know.

I know Ma liked her. She told me so. Actually, what she said was, "Luke, the woman is good for you." Ma was sparse with complements, so when she said them, she meant them.

Lucy had brought a side out of me that I didn't know existed. The strong urge to protect a woman that didn't need protecting hit me daily. I want Lucy to have everything in life I could give her. I've never felt like that before I met Lucy.

The truth was that I only responded to the advertisement for a husband, because I couldn't find any work and marrying her had seemed like the best choice. I stared at my wife in the firelight. When she was asleep like this, all of her features relaxed. She was truly the most beautiful woman I'd ever seen. I was kind of glad she liked to wear pants and overalls, because it kept the other men at arm's length until I met her.

I hoped she liked the presents I got for her. I didn't want to disappoint her in any way. I wanted to be a good husband to her.

The fire was getting lower. I got up and put a few logs on the fire. I watched it for a moment to make sure no stray flames escaped.

The other room probably needed another log or two. I carefully crossed the floor to the main room. It looked like I caught the fire just in time. I put two logs on the fire and the flames purred to life. I sat down and watched the flames.

Christmas morning would be warm whenever Lucy woke up. She was my priority. Being in our home with the woman I loved was the greatest blessing of my life, and I knew it.

"Thank you, Lord, for my life with Lucy." I whispered.

I sat there in the quiet early morning and watched the flames a little longer, before sneaking out to the barn and bringing in Lucy's Christmas present. I put a spare quilt over it, so she wouldn't see it right away. I really hoped she liked it.

I walked back to our bedroom and slid in beside my wife. Her blonde hair was in a braid. I wanted to touch her, but I didn't want to wake her up.

Lucy rolled over and put her arm on my chest. It was heaven. She wiggled closer. I couldn't help smiling. She was beyond beautiful. I laid there for several minutes, looking at the ceiling, before I felt movement beside of me.

Lucy's eyes blinked open. "Good morning."

"Good morning." I whispered.

I leaned toward her and kissed her. My heart picked up speed. My wife smiled. She reached out and touched my face. I couldn't help grinning. This had to be the best Christmas of my life.

"Merry Christmas." I whispered again.

"Merry Christmas." Lucy moved closer to me and placed her head in the crook of my arm.

"I love you, Lucy." I rubbed her arm.

"I love you, Luke Larson." Lucy kissed my chest and giggled.

Lucy

Thirty-One
31

"I got you a present." I smiled at my husband.

"You did? What did you get me?" Luke's eyes lit up.

"I can't tell you! You have to open it." I giggled.

"I thought you were my present." Luke covered my lips with his.

Time disappeared. Kissing Luke had quickly become one of my favorite pass times. He had a way of setting me on fire.

"I love you." Luke whispered.

"You already said that once this morning." I grinned.

Luke chuckled.

"Is there a rule saying, only once?" Luke brushed my hair out of my face.

I shook my head no.

"Do you have something you would like to say?" My husband whispered.

"I will have to think about it." I put my index finger to my chin.

"Think about it?" Luke scoffed.

"I'm just joshing you." I giggled.

"I know." His eyes twinkled.

"I love you." I kissed him on the lips.

"This is our first Christmas together." Luke's tone was sappier than normal.

"The first of many." I got out of bed. "Come on, I want you to open your present."

Luke chuckled and put on a shirt. I quickly got dressed and undid my braid. Luke was standing in the doorway watching me.

"What are you doing?" I ran a brush through my hair.

"Watching a beautiful woman." My husband's grin sent a blush straight to my cheeks.

"Sweet-talker." I kept brushing my hair.

"Is it working?" Luke grinned proudly.

"Maybe?" I giggled.

I quickly braided my hair again, and we headed into the main room. In the corner was a quilt covering something. I wasn't sure what was underneath. All I knew was that it wasn't there last night.

"What's that?" I pointed to the quilt.

"Your present." Luke smiled proudly.

"Do you want to go first, or do you want me to go first?" I put a hand on his forearm.

"You can open yours first." Luke stepped back.

I walked over and removed the quilt. Underneath it was a beautiful bench. It must have been what he was working on in the barn for the past few days.

"I plan on making a table and another bench, but I ran out of time." Luke stepped closer.

I ran my hands along the wood. It was soft to the touch. If this is what he could do in a few days, I wonder what he could do with more time.

"Do you like it?" Luke's tone was concerned.

I nodded my head. I turned around and wrapped my arms around him. We've been sitting on the floor and the bed since we moved in.

"It's perfect, Luke. I love it." I sat down and pulled his package from the back corner of the tree and handed both packages to him.

"Thank you." His eyes were curious. "It's heavy." He was holding the one with the tools in it.

"It is." I smiled.

He carefully slid the twine off the paper. He peeled back the paper. Luke's mouth fell open. "What did you do?"

"Do you like them?" I bit my lower lip.

Luke's fingers ran over the tools. His deep eyes met mine. He leaned over the present and pressed his warm lips to mine. When he pulled back, he had several emotions walking around his eyes.

"So you like it?" I clasped my hands together. I can't remember feeling this nervous before over a present.

Luke's fingertips ran over the tools. "It's beyond perfect." He nodded his appreciation.

I let out the breath I didn't know I was holding.

"Thank you." Luke smiled. "Although, I think you might have gotten me the better present."

"Not possible." I swallowed. "I have you."

I felt my cheeks heat. I had a hard time expressing feelings. I know most women were experts by my age, but I felt more comfortable mucking out stalls than admitting how much he meant to me.

"I love you, Sweetheart." Luke's expression matched his words.

I felt warm all over.

"You didn't have to get me two presents." He picked up the last package.

It didn't take long for Luke to reveal the sharpening set.

"I thought you might need it." I waited for him to respond.

"It's perfect, just like you." We shared another kiss.

I cuddled next to Luke, and we watched the fire flicker in the fireplace.

"I bet Beth Ann and Tommy are up." I whispered.

"Are you ready to head to the main house?" Luke rubbed my shoulder.

I nodded my head.

Luke got up and put the fires out in both rooms. That was the only thing bad about leaving our home. I put on my coat and fed the chickens while Luke saddled our horses.

I hated leaving our little home, but I wanted to see Beth Ann and Pa. Luke and I left our presents for them at the main house yesterday. I made my way into the barn.

"Are you ready to see all of your friends?" I patted my horse on the side.

My horse neighed, and I laughed.

"Ready, Sweetheart?" Luke was leading his horse out of the barn.

"Yes." I leaned closer to my horse. "Merry Christmas, girl."

My horse neighed again as I led her out of the barn. Luke closed the door behind us to keep out some of the cold. I was chilled to the bone as we arrived at the main house.

"What's going on down there?" Tommy poked his head over the loft.

"Merry Christmas, Tommy!" I smiled.

"I thought you were sleeping in our old place." Luke called up.

"I tried, but it was too quiet." Tommy complained.

I put my horse in her old stall and put the saddle in front of it.

"Get down here and help me milk the cows." Luke put his horse away.

Tommy climbed down the ladder. He ran over and gave us both a hug. I could see the excitement on his face.

"Merry Christmas!" Tommy grinned.

"Merry Christmas, kid." Luke messed up his brother's hair.

Tommy ran across the yard ahead of us. Luke and I walked at a slower pace hand in hand, enjoying every moment of Christmas morning. The door flew open.

"Merry Christmas!" Luke's Ma greeted us at the door.

"Merry Christmas!" I hugged my mother-in-law.

"Merry Christmas, Ma!" Luke sauntered over and wrapped his mother in a hug. She was pint-sized as he dwarfed over here.

"Get in here, it's cold outside!" Pa yelled from inside.

The air was full of excitement. I had spent all of my Christmases in this house. I couldn't imagine spending Christmas anywhere else. Each part of the house I grew up in was full of memories. Ma tried to teach me to sew. Pa carrying me over his head out the door. Beth Ann taking her first steps.

"You made it!" Beth Ann rushed across the room and threw her arms around me. "I didn't think you'd be able to come!" My sister gushed.

"Of course I made it. I'm not going to miss Christmas!" I hugged my sister tighter.

"Does this mean we can FINALLY open presents? Ma said we had to wait for you to show up." Tommy pointed at Luke.

"Not yet!" Ma clapped her hands. "The turkey is done. I've been keeping it warm for over an hour, hoping Lukey and Lucy would make it."

I smiled at my husband. He rolled his eyes. I knew being called Lukey was a term of endearment that he didn't care for. We each found a seat and sat down. I put my coat on the back of my chair.

"Let's pray." Pa bowed his head.

The rest of us followed suit. The smell of turkey taunted me the entire time Pa prayed. I was usually better at concentrating, but the food smelled delicious.

"Lord, we thank you for bringing us together for Christmas. We appreciate you making a way for my Lucy and Luke to be here today. We thank you for coming to the Earth as a baby and being born. Thank you for the delicious Christmas dinner and the hands that prepared it. In Jesus' name, amen." Pa lifted his head.

"Amen." I echoed.

My father's smile reached all the way to his eyes. He was starting to come alive again. After Ma died, life was hard, but Pa was getting back to himself. I didn't think that would happen again.

"Can someone pass the Christmas pudding?" I pointed to the familiar dish.

"Don't eat it all." Tommy passed it to me.

I laughed.

"Tommy, you can't say stuff like that to women-folk." Luke reprimanded him.

"It ain't womenfolk, just Lucy." Tommy shrugged.

"Tommy!" Beth Ann pointed at him. "Lucy is wom-enfolk, so is your Ma, and so is Lucy."

"Alright. Alright." Tommy held up his hand in sur-render.

I laughed.

Luke rubbed his face and scratched his head.

"It's okay." I patted my husband's leg under the table. "It's Christmas." I smiled.

Turkey was piled on a serving tray and passed around the table. It didn't take us long to finish all of the special pies, pudding, and turkey. I didn't think I could eat another bite.

"Who wants to read the Christmas story this year?" Luke's Ma asked.

"Lucy usually does." Beth Ann quipped.

I wasn't usually self-conscious, but I wasn't used to reading in front of Luke, and I didn't want to mess up any of the words. Beth Ann had the Bible in my lap before I could protest. I turned to Luke chapter 2 and began reading about the miracle of the baby that came to Earth to save us all. I choked up a little when I got to the part where Mary pondered the miracle of Jesus' birth in her heart.

"And that's why we celebrate Christmas." Beth Ann grinned.

"Yes, it is." Pa smiled.

"Can we have presents now?" Tommy complained.

"Yes, presents now." Luke's Ma laughed.

Tommy opened his presents with the enthusiasm of a child. So much had changed in a year. I couldn't wait to see what the next year brought. Before I knew it, I was hugging everyone goodnight. I knew I would remember this first Christmas with Luke as long as I lived.

"Merry Christmas, Lucy." Luke whispered to me in the wagon on our way back home.

"Merry Christmas, Luke." I leaned against him and was filled with warmth and love.

Luke

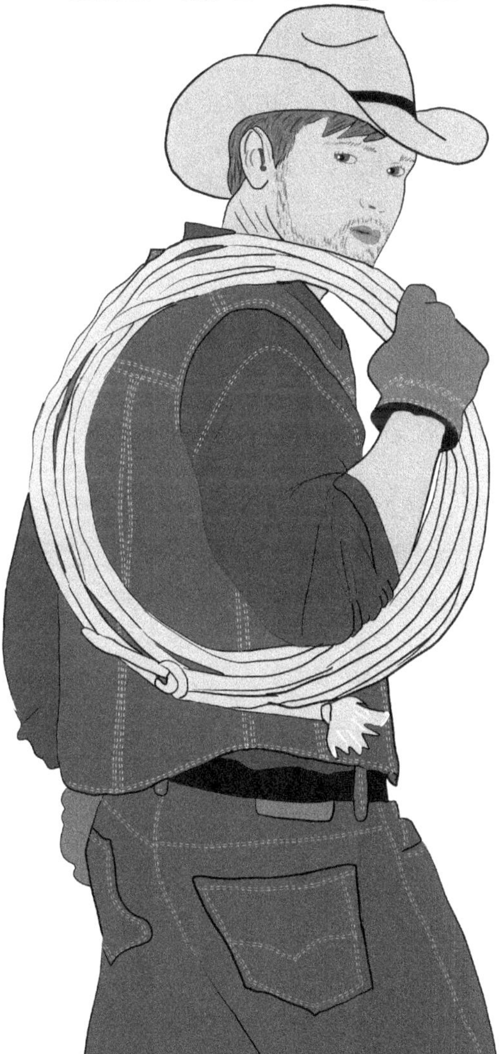

Thirty-Two
32

There was a chill in the air. I blinked twice. It was time to wake up. Lucy's blonde hair cascaded across her pillow. I didn't want to wake her. Lucy's hand was on my arm. She was perfect. She was mine. Lucy rolled away from me. I guess that was my sign to wake up for the morning.

I moved the cover and put it down around Lucy. The cold air hit my bare chest. I let out a deep breath and pulled on a shirt before walking over to the fireplace and putting a log on the fire. The flames were distorted before they welcomed the wood. The heat increased. I put my fingertips over the fire. They grew warm in seconds.

We had been snowed in the house for days. I loved being around Lucy, but I was ready for spring. I missed the sunshine. Instead, all we had was dark clouds.

"Good morning." Lucy whispered.

"Good morning." I stood up and crossed the distance between us.

Lucy smiled as I leaned over her. I bent down and kissed her on her forehead. My wife's hand touched my cheek.

"Come here." Lucy's breath hit my skin.

There was no way I could tell her no. It was quite some time before I thought about anything, but my wife. Lucy had a way of making me forget about time.

"I guess we better get up." Lucy kissed me and crawled out of bed.

"That's what I was trying to do earlier." I put my hand behind my head and watched her get dressed.

We made our way to the main room to find something to eat, but we were running low on supplies. I had more in the cellar, but I didn't want to dig it out. The horses were probably hungry.

"I better check on the horses." I put on my boots.

"Okay. Do you want some help?" Lucy yawned.

"No, I got it. I'll be right back." I put on my coat and buttoned it.

I opened the door and stared. The snow had melted in the middle of the night. I craned my neck left to right.

"Is something wrong?" Lucy put her hand on my shoulder.

"The snow melted. You want to head to the main house?" I turned around to see my wife.

"I'll get my boots on." Lucy reached for her boots.

I closed the door and breathed in the fresh air. I knew it wasn't spring yet, but the warm weather gave me hope. I whistled all the way to the barn. It didn't take me long to get the horses ready to go and feed the chickens.

"I put out the fires." Lucy rushed down the path.

"I fed the chickens." I grinned at my wife.

"Let's go." Lucy climbed up on her horse.

I closed the barn doors behind us and climbed onto my horse. The wind hit my face, and I felt alive. My horse was as excited to be going somewhere as I was.

When we reached the main house, I checked the barn, all of the chores were done. Tommy apparently earned his keep. I didn't want to go back inside just yet.

"I think I'm going to ride to town and check the mail." I got back on my horse.

"Can you pick up some extra flour and sugar? We're running low." Lucy was taking off the saddle from her horse.

"Sure." It was a good thing I brought my wallet with me.

"Have fun." Lucy waved.

I enjoyed the ride to town. I felt free again, instead of cooped up. I wasn't meant to stay indoors.

I went to the General Store first and picked up the flour and sugar.

"Thanks, Mr. Montgomery." I waved to him as I left the store.

"Bye, Mr. Larson." Mr. Montgomery called after me.

I tucked the flour and sugar into my saddlebag before walking over to check the mail.

"Here you go, Mr. Larson." The postmaster handed me an envelope. "That's it."

"Thank you, sir." I waved as I left the building.

I walked to my horse as I opened up the letter. It was addressed to me. I didn't recognize the handwriting.

Luke,

I know it's been a while, but I need you to come. I'll explain when you arrive.

Uncle Billy

Enclosed was enough fare to get on the next train. I frowned. The letter was vague. I didn't like it. Uncle Billy was Ma's brother. He had done a lot for me and my family when Pa died. I folded up the letter and put it in my pants pocket. I needed to talk to Lucy.

I headed back home. I didn't know what to do. Family was everything, but Lucy was family too. I didn't like the idea of leaving her.

Lucy

Thirty-Three
33

"Lucy!" My sister wrapped her hands around me.

I hugged Beth Ann back. "It's only been a few days." I laughed.

"A long few days!" My sister made a face. "There has been nothing to do."

"Well, the snow finally melted." I turned towards the window.

I wish we had windows at home. Luke promised me that he would put some in when it warmed up. There hadn't been time before winter hit. I wanted two in the main room and one in the bedroom.

"Or it might snow again." Beth Ann huffed.

"You could always stay in the barn." I teased.

Beth Ann's mouth fell open. "What? With Tommy? I can't do that! It smells out there, and he snores! I went out there one morning to feed the chickens; it's a miracle the animals didn't run away, he was so loud."

I laughed. "Please tell me you have been taking care of my animals every day."

"Tommy has." Beth Ann nodded. "He said Luke threatened him."

I chuckled. "It sounds like Luke."

Luke didn't raise a word to me, but when it came to Tommy, he had no qualms about threatening him or yelling at him. I missed Luke already. He had only left for town a few minutes ago. I probably should have gone with him, but I missed Beth Ann and Pa.

"Sit down. I'll get you some coffee and cookies." Beth Ann patted the table.

"Cookies sound wonderful. We ran out a few days ago." I wasn't much of a cook.

We still needed a proper stove. All we had was the fireplace. I could cook eggs on it and chili, but not much more.

Beth Ann chattered so fast, I had a hard time keeping up. I was lucky to nod in the right places. Millie joined us.

When Beth Ann finally stopped for a few minutes, I made my escape to the barn. I missed my animals. I breathed in the barn smell. It felt like home here.

"Did you guys miss me?" I greeted each animal.

I heard someone on the path. I walked out of the barn. I saw Luke coming up the path. My heart beat faster. I missed him. He pulled into the barn and hopped down.

"Hey Sweetheart." He leaned down and kissed me.

Something was off in his tone and the way he held himself. I couldn't place it. Sadness had replaced the excitement he left with this morning.

"What's wrong?" I scowled.

A slight smiled tugged in the corner of his lips. "Just like that, you think something is wrong?"

"Luke." I crossed my arms.

My husband pulled an envelope out of his pocket and handed it to me. I read the note. I wasn't sure what to make of it.

"I think I ought to go." His liquid brown eyes met mine. "I don't want to leave you though." He let out a deep breath and readjusted his stance.

I glanced at the letter again. I handed it back. My heart felt like it was breaking. I didn't want Luke to leave. I was used to seeing him every day. It was more than that... I loved him.

"Do what you think is best." I turned on my heals and started to walk away.

I couldn't stand there and talk about Luke leaving. I felt tears on my cheeks. Luke was my world. I didn't want him to leave, but I knew how he felt about his Uncle Billy. Luke was a loyal man. He was all about taking care of family.

"Hey." Luke came running after me.

I tried to compose myself, but a few more tears escaped. Luke stepped in front of me and blocked my escape.

"Say the word and I won't go." Luke touched my cheek.

"You have to go." I whispered.

"He didn't ask for Tommy, so he can stay and help out with the chores. I will probably only be gone a week or two." My husband's voice was very convincing.

"I know." I blinked rapidly, hoping the tears would stop.

Luke stepped closer and pulled me to his chest. I could hear his heart beat. It only reminded me that he was about to leave. I wish he had never gone to town. I wish we had stayed at home.

"That's it, I'm not going." Luke rubbed my back.

"Your Uncle Billy wouldn't have asked you to come if he didn't need you." I mumbled into his shirt.

"I know." Luke's hot breath hit my face.

"When are you leaving?" I whispered.

"A train is leaving tomorrow. I should probably be on it." Luke's voice was full of remorse.

"I understand." I stepped back from my husband.

"Do you?" Luke's eyes were full of regret.

A sob escaped my lips as I ran out of the barn. I ran to the shack we had spent the first part of our marriage and let the tears fall. I didn't want Luke to see me cry, but my heart was too heavy to hold the tears at bay.

Luke

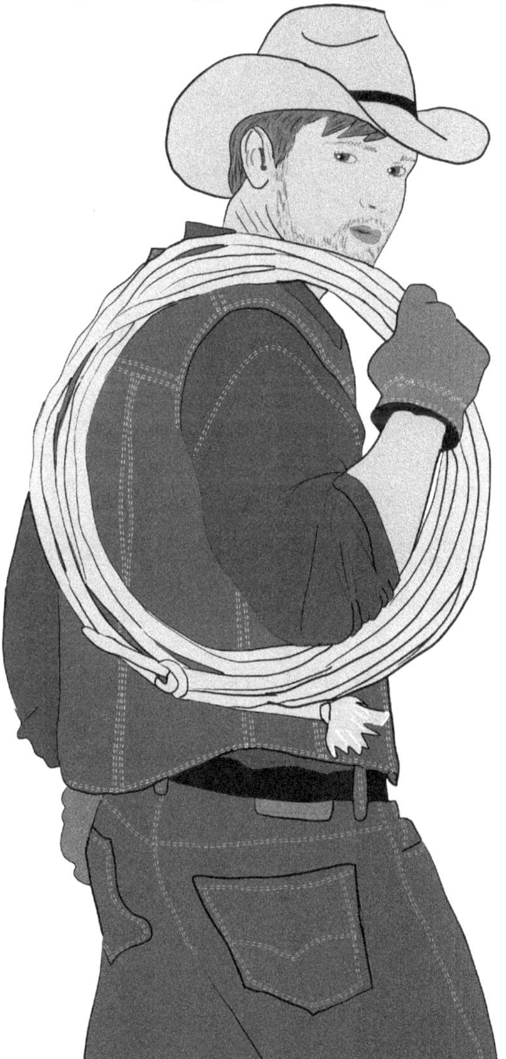

Thirty-Four
34

I hated watching her walk out the door. I turned around and punched the stacked hay behind me. I punched it again. It didn't take away the pain I felt about leaving Lucy behind.

I wish I had never seen the letter. I crumbled it up and put it in my pocket. Family was supposed to show up when no one else did. Pa would have gone. I leaned against the hay.

My horse started getting antsy. I should have taken care of him right away. Usually, Lucy stayed around and talked when I came back from going places. This time she had left the barn in tears and there was nothing I could do about it.

I closed my eyes and fought off the anger. I had to pull it together. I wasn't a kid like Tommy. I was a grown man with grown responsibilities. I brushed down my horse, and put my horse away. I made sure he had enough food.

"I wish you had an answer." I patted my favorite horse's head.

A soft neigh told me good luck. I scowled as I walked into the main house. I would have to tell Ma what was going on after telling Lucy. It felt like a double whammy.

I opened the door. Lucy was nowhere to be seen. My stomach hurt when I thought about leaving.

"Lukey!" Ma ran over and hugged me. "Hi, Ma." I hugged her back.

"I think Ma missed you." Tommy laughed.

I should have been happy, but the fact that I was leaving tainted everything. I pulled out the envelope. I handed it over to my mother. I couldn't get the words out.

"What's this?" Ma took it and started reading it. "I hope Billy is alright." Ma put her hand to her chest.

"What does it say, Ma?" Tommy tried to see the letter.

"Uncle Billy needs Luke to come help him for a little while." Ma put the letter on the table.

"Can I go too?" Tommy was excited. "I could see all of my friends again."

"No, he only sent enough fare for me to come." I folded my arms.

"What did Lucy say?" Beth Ann was concerned.

That was a question I didn't want to answer.

"I'm sure Lucy understands that we have to step up when family is involved." Lucy's Pa spoke up from the corner.

I don't think she did, or she wouldn't have left the barn earlier. I didn't want to leave this farm. It had become home. I didn't miss the town I came from, because Lucy was here.

"Sit down and I will get you something to eat." Ma patted the table.

I sat down, because I couldn't think of anything else to do. Lucy was hurt. How did I fix it?

I had to go help Uncle Billy. He wouldn't have written me a letter unless it was important. Fare wasn't cheap either.

The only thing I could think of was to go and do my best to hurry back home as soon as possible. I was a hard worker. I'm sure I could get back home in a week.

"Your favorite." Ma put a plate of cookies and a mug of coffee in front of me.

"Thanks, Ma." I smiled at her.

It wasn't my Ma's fault that I had to leave. I picked up a cookie. It smelled fresh.

The door rattled and opened. Lucy walked in and sat down beside me. I could feel her pain, but there was nothing I could do.

"What do you think about Luke going to visit Uncle Billy?" Tommy was grinning.

"Tommy, eat this." Beth Ann stuffed a cookie in his mouth to shut him up.

Thank you, I mouthed at my sister-in-law.

Lucy

Thirty-Five

35

The alarm clock went off. It was a painful reminder that Luke was leaving today. We usually woke up and took care of the animals without needing an alarm.

Luke's long arm turned off the clock. Dread was in the air. We both felt it.

The normal sparkle in my husband's eyes has been missing since yesterday. Luke and I quietly got ready to go. It hurt to speak.

"I'll go get the horses ready." Luke's voice was full of sadness.

"Okay." I nodded my head.

I let out the breath I had been holding when the door closed behind him. Luke needed fare to get home. I knew Billy gave him fare to get there, but I wanted to make sure he was coming home to me.

I dug in the trunk in my room and pulled out a coffee can. I carefully removed the bills he would need to get back home and added a few more just in case something happened. I didn't want him out there stranded.

I put out both fires and headed to the barn. The sun was just barely starting to rise. It should have given me hope for a new day, but instead my heart hurt.

"Here." Luke quietly handed me the reins to my horse.

"Thank you." I put my foot in the stirrup and swung my leg over the saddle.

Being in a saddle was my favorite place, but I wished I was back in bed and this day wasn't happening. My horse already knew the way to the main house by heart. Tommy had most of the chores done by the time we arrived.

"Thanks, Tommy." Luke patted him on the back.

Luke wasn't usually that nice to his brother. I guess he would miss him too. Luke gave me a sad look that tore up my already broken heart.

"Breakfast is ready!" Beth Ann called from the front porch.

"Go inside, Tommy. We'll be in, in a minute." Luke kept milking the cow.

Tommy ran to the house.

The silence between us held weight. There wasn't anything left to do, but wait on Luke. I wasn't going to let him out of my sight until I saw him get on the train.

Luke sang to the cow. I didn't realize how much I would miss Luke until I watched him do everything today for the last time. It was like I was ripping one tooth out at a time.

Luke finished milking the cow, and the two of us headed inside. Breakfast was usually a happy occasion. Today, we were all much quieter than normal. I wasn't the only one dreading Luke's upcoming absence.

"I guess I better go if I'm going to make the train." Luke stood up.

"I'll miss you, Lukey." Millie hugged her son.

"I'll miss you too, Ma." Luke hugged her back.

"Are you sure that I can't come?" Tommy stepped closer to his brother.

"Yes, I'm sure." Luke gave him a hug.

"I wish I could go too." Tommy's voice was strained.

"Take care of the animals and listen to Ma while I'm gone." Luke pointed at his brother.

"I will." Tommy nodded.

"Bye." Luke waved and walked out the door as a chorus of goodbyes followed him.

The trip into town wasn't nearly as long as I would have liked. I didn't want to miss one second with my husband. Part of me wanted to go with him. Maybe I should?

If I did leave with Luke, there would be no one left here to make sure the farm kept going. Tommy could take care of the animals, but there was more to running a farm than that. Pa was almost healed, but he wasn't the same as he had been a few weeks ago.

Luke and I tied up our horses. I followed Luke as he purchased a ticket. Letting Luke go had to be the hardest thing I've done in my life.

"I'm…" I licked my bottom lip. "…going to miss you." It hurt to say.

"Me too." Luke stepped closer.

"I'm not sure how to do this." I hugged myself.

Being this weak made me mad. I was usually stronger than this. We hadn't been married long enough for me to react this way.

"Hey, it should only be a week or two at most." Luke closed the rest of the distance between us and wrapped his arms around me.

Having him this close made me miss him more, and he wasn't even gone. I thought about all the ways my life had changed since Luke walked into my life. The thought of living without him hurt more than it should have.

I put the money in Luke's hand.

"What's this for?" He scowled.

"I want to make sure you come home to me." I touched his face.

"I should say no." Luke folded up the money.

"If your Uncle Billy pays your way back, we'll put it in the coffee can." I wasn't sure what to do with my hands. I finally put them in my pocket.

"I don't want to go." Luke's voice cracked.

"I know." I nodded.

"I wish you could come with me." Luke's eyes searched mine.

"Me too." I let out a deep breath.

"I won't be long." Luke murmured in my ear.

"I know." A tear escaped.

"I love you." Luke wiped it away.

"I love you, too." I whispered.

The train whistled.

"I have to go now." Pain was in my husband's eyes.

"Stay safe." I let go of him.

"I'll do my best." Luke bent down and kissed me goodbye.

I didn't expect him to do that in public.

"I miss you already." Luke whispered as he backed away from me.

"Write me." I waved.

"I will." My husband waved back.

Watching Luke get on the train was like watching my heart leave the station. I waved to him until the train was out of sight. Love wasn't supposed to feel like this.

Luke

Thirty-Six
36

The train came to a stop. If I were home right now, we'd be having dinner at the main house. Tommy would be telling us stories that got on my nerves and Lucy would be shaking her head. Then we would be going home and... I missed my wife.

I picked up my bag off the seat next to me and got off the train. I shielded my eyes. I didn't have time to tell Uncle Billy that I was coming, but it wasn't too far from his house.

"Luke? Is that you?" Doug walked towards me.

We had gone to school together.

"Yeah, it's me." I hugged him and patted him on the back.

"Where have you been?" Doug put his hand around his suspenders.

"I got married out of town. Uncle Billy said he needed me, so I came back for a spell." It was nice to see a friendly face.

"Married? You? You're joshing me." Doug chuckled.

"No, her name is Lucy. She's prettier than a sunset." I grinned, thinking about her.

"Good for you." Doug turned around. "I don't see your Uncle Billy. Do you need a ride over to his place?"

"That'd be great." I grinned.

"You're in luck. I brought my wagon." Doug patted me on the back.

"Thanks, Doug. I appreciate this." I climbed up in his wagon.

"So this wife?" Doug grinned at me.

"Yeah?" I laughed at the way he said it.

"Does she have a sister? If the poor sap went for you, I might have a chance with her sister." Doug flicked the reins.

I shook my head.

"No, sister?" Doug nodded his head. "Too bad."

"No, she has a sister, but she's too young for you." I rolled my eyes.

"Shame." Doug nodded his head. "How young is too young?"

"Shut up." I shoved him.

Doug chuckled. "All I'm saying is if she is half as pretty as you say her sister is, write me a letter when she comes of age. If I'm still single..." Doug held his hand out and let the sentence fade away.

"Yeah, yeah. I hear you." I chuckled.

Doug always had a way of making me laugh. It didn't take us long to fall into an old rhythm. He stopped the wagon in front of Uncle Billy's house. I hopped out of the wagon.

"Thanks for the ride." I patted the seat twice and grabbed my bag.

"Old Luke Larson, a married man. What a shame." Doug shook his head.

"You should try it sometime." I gave as good as I got.

"Nah, I'm not ready for that. Let me know when the sister is old enough to start courting. I might be ready then." There was a glimmer in his eye as he snapped the reins and left.

I shook my head as I made my way to Uncle Billy's front door. The door flew open before I could knock. It was my Aunt Lorraine.

"Luke! I am so glad you came." She hugged me. "Billy! Guess who is here?"

"Hello, Aunt Lorraine. Ma sends her love." I walked in and she closed the door behind me. "What's going on?"

"I'll let Billy explain it." Aunt Lorraine's expression changed to bittersweet.

"Luke, you came." Uncle Billy walked towards me, covered in sawdust.

"Yes, sir." I nodded.

"Good of you to come." He held out his hand.

I shook it. "Yes, sir."

"Come on." He waved for me to follow him. "You'll see what we are up against."

"Yes, sir." I grabbed my bag and followed him.

I did my best not to think about Lucy, but it was impossible. We would be having dinner about now. Ma would have the table set. Beth Ann would be talking up a storm. Tommy would be correcting her. Lucy's Pa would have been taking it all in.

I hoped this trip would go faster than expected. I was willing to work long hours to get the job finished faster. A strong breeze whipped through the room and tickled my throat when Uncle Billy lifted the quilt covering the door to go into the kitchen. I coughed and hurried to catch up.

Uncle Billy led me to the kitchen. A large tree had crashed through the roof. Someone had cleaned around it, but I could see the sky. I was speechless.

"I asked around. Every quote I got was more than I could afford. I have just enough to buy the supplies, but as you can see, I can't do this myself." Uncle Billy put his hands on his hips and looked up.

"At least it hasn't rained!" Aunt Lorraine called from the other room.

"The kids are at her mother's house, so I've been cutting off the smaller limbs and putting them into the firewood pile, but I've had to ride to the next town over to work at the factory. If I miss a day, they'll give my job away." Uncle Billy explained.

I'd tried to get a job at the factory Uncle Billy worked at, but they had a waiting list for jobs there. Most of the men that worked there have been working there since before they were my age.

"Do you think you can fix it?" Uncle Billy turned to me.

I nodded my head.

"Good." Uncle Billy patted me. "I'll show you where I put the supplies."

I followed Uncle Billy out to the barn. There was a pile of lumber right inside of the door. I held onto my suspenders. This was going to be some work.

"Do you think you can help me get the tree cut before nightfall?" I turned to my uncle.

"We can give it a go." Uncle Billy patted me on the back. "I missed you, Luke."

I didn't miss Uncle Billy at all. I missed Lucy. I nodded my head instead.

"Ma says hello." I walked over to the tool table and picked up a saw.

"Does she like it out there?" Uncle Billy was curious.

"She seems to. Lucy and Beth Ann give her run of the kitchen." I smiled.

"Lucy. That's the woman you married, right?" Uncle Billy picked up the big saw.

"That's right, sir." I nodded my head.

"She don't care that your Ma is in charge of the kitchen?" Uncle Billy scowled.

"No, sir." I chuckled. "Lucy prefers to be outdoors with me."

"Sounds odd. I bet she wears britches too." Uncle Billy laughed like it was a joke.

"Actually, she does." I smiled.

"What a shame." Uncle Billy shook his head.

"I like her just fine." I felt the need to stand up for my wife.

"Is that so?" Uncle Billy eyed me for a moment.

I nodded.

A slow smile spread across his face. He nudged my arm like old men do. I couldn't help laughing as I left the barn.

Uncle Billy helped me attack the tree. It took us a couple of hours, but we had it cleared out of the kitchen. We had to finish by lamplight.

"Thank you, son, for all of your help." Uncle Billy patted me on the back.

"You helped us when we needed it." I put the saw back on the tool table in the barn.

"That's what family is for." Uncle Billy walked to the barn door, and waited for me.

Lucy

Thirty-Seven
37

I walked inside of the barn. The wind shifted and the smell of manure irritated my nose. I started to gag. I ran behind the barn and threw up. It didn't make any sense.

I got a bucket and pumped the water until the bucket was full. I carried it back to where I threw up and poured the bucket of water on it. I did it a few more times before I sat the bucket beside the pump.

"Lucy, do you need me to do anything?" Tommy walked inside of the barn.

I swallowed. "Could you muck out the stalls?"

"Okay." Tommy got to work.

I quickly fed the animals. "Thank you, Tommy."

"You're welcome." Tommy was hard at work.

I walked out of the barn and leaned on the side of it. This was not normal. It didn't feel right to have

Tommy doing my work, but I wasn't up to spending the day in the barn.

I didn't feel up to dinner. Without Luke around, this day seemed doomed from the start. I headed into the main house.

"Lucy, you look a little pale. Are you okay?" Millie was visibly concerned.

"I think I'm going to head home. I don't feel up to working today." I hated to say it, but the way I was feeling, there was no way I could finish the things I was planning on finishing.

"Let me get you some toast. That will make you feel better." Millie cut up some bread on the counter.

"You're probably just Luke sick." Beth Ann grinned.

"Maybe?" I frowned.

It felt like more than that. Millie put the toast in front of me. I felt a little better after I ate it.

"I'll pack you up some bread to take with you." Millie put the remainder of the loaf in a cloth and wrapped it up.

"Thank you." I took the bread and headed back to the dreaded barn to saddle up my horse.

I managed to get out of the barn without losing the contents of my stomach again. The ride home was cold and lonely. I missed Luke. Maybe Beth Ann had been right?

I took care of my horse. When I went to close the barn door, there was a folded paper tucked between the cracks of the wood. Lucy was written on the outside of it. My heart beat faster. I picked it up and unfolded it.

Lucy,

I never wanted to be in two places at once so badly in my life. I already miss you. Sorry, I didn't mean to get all sappy.

I love you,

Luke

I read the letter twice. I folded it up and leaned on the wall beside of the barn door.

"I love you too, Luke." I whispered.

I closed my eyes and tears flew down my cheeks. I know he had to help his uncle, but I missed him. The wind whipped through the barn. I wiped my tears away and headed into my house.

The quiet never sounded so loud. I stared at the fireplace. Luke would have started it for me. Sadness seeped in.

I walked to my bedroom and put Luke's note on the bed. The quilts were still messed up from when we left this morning. I started the fire in the bedroom and walked to the main room and started a fire in the fireplace.

My stomach gurgled. I ran outside to the outhouse and threw up. That's when I remembered I forgot the bread in my saddlebag.

I headed back to the barn, patted my horse, and took the bread back inside the house. This day was a lost cause. I laid down on the bed and fell asleep with the half loaf of bread in my arm.

Luke

Thirty-Eight
38

I woke up coughing. My chest hurt. My throat hurt. This was the last day of being here, then I could go back home to Lucy. I missed holding her. I missed the look in her eyes when she wasn't expecting me to walk through the door. I missed covering her lips with mine. My dreams were filled with my wife, but they weren't enough.

I coughed again. I tried to swallow. My throat was swollen. I just needed to get through today. I got dressed and headed over to eat my breakfast. I had another coughing fit in the middle of eating.

"Are you okay, Luke?" Aunt Lorraine was concerned.

I nodded my head. "I think so."

I started coughing again. My chest was starting to hurt from coughing so much. I would be home soon, I told myself again. I was distracted by my aching body. I didn't usually feel like this. I wasn't that old. I shouldn't feel like someone had squeezed the life out of me.

I finished my work and went to get a drink of water. I didn't feel up to eating. My throat was too tight. I went back and laid down in the barn loft. I had to get better. I need to get back to Lucy.

My eyes felt hot under my skin, when I closed them. Just lay still and it will go away. You'll be fine. I tried to make myself feel better, but it didn't work.

I went into another coughing fit. My throat was getting tighter. I started shivering. I tugged a blanket over me. My eyes were so hot. How could I be so hot and cold at the same time? My eyes closed. I was on the edge of blissful sleep. Then I started coughing. My throat was raw. I turned on my side.

"Luke, why are you held up in here?" Uncle Billy called from the ground.

"I'm sorry... can't." My eyes fluttered open and closed.

"Go get the doctor." Uncle Billy spoke.

"Yes, sir." Jr. answered his father.

"I don't need a doctor." I started coughing almost uncontrollably.

"Son, I don't think I can send you home like this." Uncle Billy had climbed up the ladder.

Dread filled my soul. I was so close to being with Lucy. I wanted to go home, but I didn't want her to catch this. I closed my eyes. Every time I started to fall asleep, I started coughing.

Somewhere among the coughing, I fell asleep. Aunt Lorraine woke me up with a bowl of soup. The warm liquid felt good on my throat. I drifted off to sleep.

"Where is the young man at?" An unfamiliar voice came from the ground.

"He's up in the loft." Uncle Billy's voice echoed through the barn.

I couldn't keep my eyes open; they physically hurt. I started coughing again. I tried to listen to what they were saying.

"Do you think he can come here, so I can examine him?" The unfamiliar voice was loud.

"Luke, do you think you can make it down here?" Uncle Billy called from the ground.

"I can try." I muttered as I rolled over.

I dropped my quilt to the ground. I didn't think I could make the trek back up here once I made it down. It was all I could do to hold on to the ladder. I sat down on the edge of the wagon.

"You've gotten worse." Uncle Billy put his hands on his hips.

"Open up." The doctor ordered.

I opened up.

"It looks like you're under quarantine, son." The doctor stood up.

"Quarantine?" I blinked.

My throat ached to even say the word. I knew I was sick, but I wasn't sure what kind of sick would put me in quarantine. It was all I could do not to fall off the wagon sitting up.

"He has Scarlet Fever. He needs to be kept separate from the rest of the house." The doctor got in his bag and removed a few packets. "Give him these, once in the morning and once at night. I'll be back to check on him next week."

"Next week? Doc, I'm supposed to be going back home tomorrow." It hurt to keep my eyes open.

"It can't be helped." The doctor shook his head.

"Doc, can I still go to work? I can't lose my job." Billy was concerned.

"Sure, as long as you don't touch him." The doctor nodded his head.

"Thank you for coming, Doc." Uncle Billy patted the doctor on the shoulder and walked out of the barn with him.

I closed my eyes and tried not to fall over. There was no way I could climb up the ladder. I heard footsteps.

"Tough break, son." Billy had come back into the barn.

"Can you write to Lucy and let her know that I won't be home?" I held my throat.

"Sure, son." Billy agreed.

"I don't think I can climb up to the loft." I got off the wagon and walked over and picked up the quilt.

"You can sleep in this empty stall." Billy opened a door and put some fresh hay in it.

"Thanks, Uncle Billy." I collapsed on the floor and covered up with a blanket.

I was exhausted. Scarlet Fever wasn't anything to mess with. I didn't want Lucy to get sick. Maybe the Doc was right? It was better to lie here and not move.

Everything hurt. It was all I could do to stay still. I had to get better. Sleep is what I needed. Sleep would make me feel better.

Lucy loves me. She said she would miss me. I needed to get better, so I would make it back home to Lucy.

I wish Lucy was here. I could almost feel her holding my hand. Home was calling my name. I was supposed to be leaving. Somewhere in the middle of my thoughts, I fell asleep. Lucy was in my dreams.

Lucy

Thirty-Nine
39

Luke should be home by now. I finished up my chores. I walked into the main house. The smell of something sweet flew into my nostrils. Laughter hit my ears as I walked inside. Beth Ann was helping Luke's Ma make pies.

"These are going to be the best pies I have ever made." Beth Ann's voice was proud.

"How many pies have you made?" Luke's Ma tilted her head.

"Three, counting this one." Beth Ann giggled. "That's why it will be the best." She giggled again.

"Practice makes perfect." Luke's Ma opened the oven and put two pies inside.

"Lucy!" Beth Ann finally saw me. "What are you doing here?"

"I am going to head to town and see if the mail came. I thought I would see if you want to come too."

Beth Ann took off her apron. "YES!" She ran out the door.

"Do you need anything while I'm in town?" I turned to my mother-in-law.

She shook her head.

"Okay." I turned on my heels.

Beth Ann chattered all the way to town. I managed to nod in the right places, but the only thing I could think about was Luke. He'd been gone almost six weeks. It was only supposed to be for a week or two. My mind was racing. That was why I was on my way to town. I was hoping there was a letter. I checked last week too, but Luke hadn't written me.

"I'll be at the General Store." Beth Ann ran off before I could say a word.

I tied off the horses and walked inside of the nearest building. I was tempted to get on a train and see what was taking him so long. It was a lot of money one way and back just to see what was going on. It seemed foolish to waste that much money when Luke would be coming home any day now.

I walked into the postmaster's building.

"Lucy, there are a few letters for you. Do you know a Billy?" He pushed three envelopes toward me.

"Luke had to go help his Uncle Billy. It's probably about that." I took the envelopes.

The first one was from Luke.

Lucy,

I miss you already. I hope Tommy is helping out. If he isn't, threaten him and I will tan his hide when I get home. Uncle Billy had a tree fall on his house. We cut up the tree yesterday. I put a patch on the roof today. I think it will hold. I should be home in a few days.

I love you!

Your Husband

I checked the date. It was from almost six weeks ago! Where was Luke? I opened the next one from Billy.

Lucy,

Luke's real sick. Doc said he has to stay here for a spell. When he's better, we'll send him home.

Billy

I checked the date. It was from about five weeks ago — WHAT HAPPENED? I've checked the mail like clockwork. Why was I just now receiving the letters? I opened the next letter.

Lucy,

Luke has Scarlet Fever. He is under quarantine. I don't know when he will be home. Doc says he can't go nowhere, cause he will make other folks sick. We're taking real good care of Luke, so don't you worry none.

Billy

I checked the date. That was four weeks ago. WHY WAS I JUST GETTING THESE LETTERS NOW?

"Is everything alright?" The postmaster was concerned.

"No, sir. I need to send a telegram." I took a page off the counter and started jotting down my message to Billy in pencil.

Luke

Forty
40

I felt like I was dying. I wanted to die. My throat was aching. I touched the outside of my throat. It felt fine on the outside of my throat, but touching it made the inside of my throat throb. It was like an itch that needed scratched.

"Sit up." Aunt Lorraine instructed.

I didn't want to sit up. I didn't want to do anything. I wanted to be home with Lucy. I was floating between anger for my circumstances and a desire to see my sweet Lucy.

I managed to sit up.

"Swallow this." Aunt Lorraine handed me the cup.

I cringed. It was apple cider vinegar again. I opened my mouth and wished my taste buds would stop working. I swallowed. My throat was in pain as I swallowed the watered-down apple cider vinegar tea.

"Here." Aunt Lorraine handed me another cup with just water in it.

I took a drink of the cup. I wiggled my tongue in the water. It helped, but it didn't.

"Lay back down. I will check on you in a bit." Aunt Lorraine gave me a kind smile.

I closed my eyes and listened to the footsteps walk away. I wanted to die. I had to live. My body was so worn out from the sickness, my brain didn't want to work properly. I coughed..

Fix me God. Please fix me. I need to be back with Lucy. My thought became lucid, and I didn't know anything else until I was woken up to swallow warm chicken broth.

I fell asleep until I heard someone open the barn door. I didn't know how long I had been out. I opened my mouth.

I couldn't talk. My throat hurt so much.

"Luke, you got a letter." Aunt Lorraine put the letter on my blanket.

I pushed myself up and stared at the envelope. I could hardly see straight. I blinked twice. My throat was throbbing.

"I'll go get you some more soup." Aunt Lorraine stepped back.

"Thank you." I croaked.

The letter was from Lucy. I swallowed and opened the letter. I blinked until I could see straight.

Luke,

I hope you are getting better. I wish you were home. I have so much to tell you. I love you with all of my heart.

You are a good man, Luke. You are strong. Fight this and come home to us... to me.

I miss you.

Your wife, Lucy

I had a tear trickle down my cheek. I rolled over. I didn't want anyone to see me cry. I had to get back to Lucy.

There was a knock on the door. I rolled back over. A man walked in with a black bag.

"Hello, Mr. Larson. I am here to look at your throat. I hear it's still hurting." The Doc was back.

The man put his hat on the chair by the door. He didn't seem any happier to be here than I was to be sick. Another week must have passed. He's been stopping by once a week since I got sick.

"Thanks for coming, Doc." I coughed into my hand.

He pulled out a wooden stick and put down his bag. "Open your mouth."

I opened up my mouth.

"I know it probably doesn't feel like it, but your throat looks a little better." The doctor set the stick aside.

"Can you fix me, Doc?" I stared at him hopefully.

"Keep taking your medicine. I have a feeling you've seen the worst of it." The Doc pulled out a few more packets of medicine. "I'm going to leave these inside with your aunt and uncle."

"Thank you, Doc. I appreciate you coming out here to check on me. How much do I owe you?" I hated to ask the question, but I paid my bills.

"Billy has already taken care of the bill. You can square it up with him." The doctor stood up. "I'll check on you next week."

"Thanks, Doc." I laid back down and held the letter to my chest.

Lucy missed me. I had to get home to her. I was glad she wasn't sick, but I missed her so much.

The barn door opened again.

"I brought your soup." Aunt Lorraine sat it down beside of me and picked up my last bowl.

"Thank you." I mumbled.

"You're welcome, Luke. I hope you start feeling better soon." Aunt Lorraine left the barn.

I had to get better. Lucy needed me. I made sure I emptied the bowl this time.

I read the letter again. My finger stopped on where Lucy said she loved me. I missed her so much.

I laid down and put the letter beside my head. The horses moved in their stalls. I wiped the sweat from my brow.

I'm glad I told Tommy to stay. I wouldn't have wanted him getting sick either. If it was my choice between me, Tommy, or Lucy, I would have chosen me to go through this.

"I love you, Lucy." I touched the letter.

I closed my eyes and fell into a deep sleep.

Lucy

Forty-One
41

I saw a horse coming up the path. I shielded my eyes. We weren't expecting anyone. The glare of the sun shifted. My mouth fell open. It was my husband, Luke.

My heart started beating rapidly as I started walking toward the barn. The horse came to a stop by the barn, before I arrived. It was really Luke. It wasn't a dream.

I walked inside of the barn in time to see him put the horse in a stall. He latched the gate behind the horse without seeing me. I came up behind him and threw my arms around him.

"Luke!" I hugged him tighter.

His warm body shifted, and he pulled me closer. My husband buried his head in my neck. My hat fell off and my hair fell onto my shoulders.

"I missed you." Luke's warm voice whispered in my ear.

"I missed you more." It was all I could do not to bawl my eyes out.

"I doubt that." He rubbed my back before leaning his forehead against mine.

I couldn't hold back the tears. I started crying. I put my head against his chest. I didn't realize how much I wanted him around, until I had to live without him. Maybe want was the wrong word?

I needed Luke. I didn't want to need anyone, but being with Luke made my heart complete. Luke put his hands on either side of my face.

"Hey, don't cry, Sweetheart." He rubbed my tears away with his thumbs.

I managed to cough back the tears. My eyes were still wet. Luke froze. His eyes went down. He took a step back and stared at me.

"Are you... you...?" Luke stumbled.

I hadn't been with child for long. It was hard to tell when I wore baggie shirts like today. Millie, Tommy, Pa and Beth Ann still hadn't noticed. It took Luke two seconds of being home to realize the secret I had been hiding from the rest of the family.

I nodded my head.

"How long?" Luke put his hand gently on my stomach.

"Right before you left." I smiled shyly.

"Oh, Luce... I would never have left." Luke closed his eyes and shook his head. "I'm sorry, Sweetheart." He stepped closer and kissed my temple.

"How are you feeling?" I whispered.

"Doc said I'm no longer contagious. My throat isn't sore anymore." Luke whispered.

"I was about to come after you." I confessed.

"You wouldn't have." Luke chuckled.

"Ask Millie and Beth Ann. I was giving it one more week." I nodded.

Luke put his hand on my stomach again. "We're a Pa and Ma."

I touched his cheek. He felt perfect. The longing in my heart was deeper than I ever imagined. Somehow, he had taken over my heart when I wasn't looking.

Luke pressed his lips to mine. I felt like I was thirsty for water after working all day. I couldn't get enough of his touch. When Luke broke our kiss, his eyes held mine. Our souls said words that our lips could not.

"Luke! Luke! You're home!" Tommy ran in and threw his arms around his brother.

"Hey Tommy! Thanks for helping hold down the fort while I was gone." Luke patted him twice on the back.

"Sure, no problem. I'm sorry you were sick." Tommy shifted his weight.

"Yeah. Me too." Luke's gaze met mine.

"But you're all better now?" Tommy's concern was evident in his voice.

"A little tired, but I'm as good as new. I need you to do me a favor and take this horse back to Mr. Turnbull tomorrow." My husband pointed to the horse in the stall.

"Sure thing, Luke." Tommy nodded. "You're right on time. Dinner is in a few minutes."

"I'll be right there. Give me a minute with Lucy." Luke's eyes were on my face.

"Okay." Tommy backed out of the barn.

Luke stepped closer. "Does Tommy know about the baby?"

I shook my head no. "You're the first."

"Thanks, Sweetheart, for waiting to tell me first." Luke whispered before kissing me again. "They've got to be blind."

I giggled.

"You're glowing." Luke grinned.

"Only because you're home." I squeezed him and laid my hand on his chest.

"Can we tell them now?" Luke breathed.

"Okay." I laughed again.

It had been weeks since I laughed. It felt strange. The happiness I felt was a huge relief. I didn't realize how much Luke's absence had been weighing on me until he returned home.

"Good, because I can't wait to tell them." Luke kissed my temple.

We walked to the main house hand in hand. Life was perfect again with Luke at home with me. I stared up at him. I was sure stars were in my eyes. My husband opened the door and smiled at me.

I had no doubt in my mind that Luke was going to be an amazing father. I couldn't wait to move on to the next step in our lives. Soon, we would be teaching our baby to ride horses and take care of the land. I had so much hope for the future.

Luke

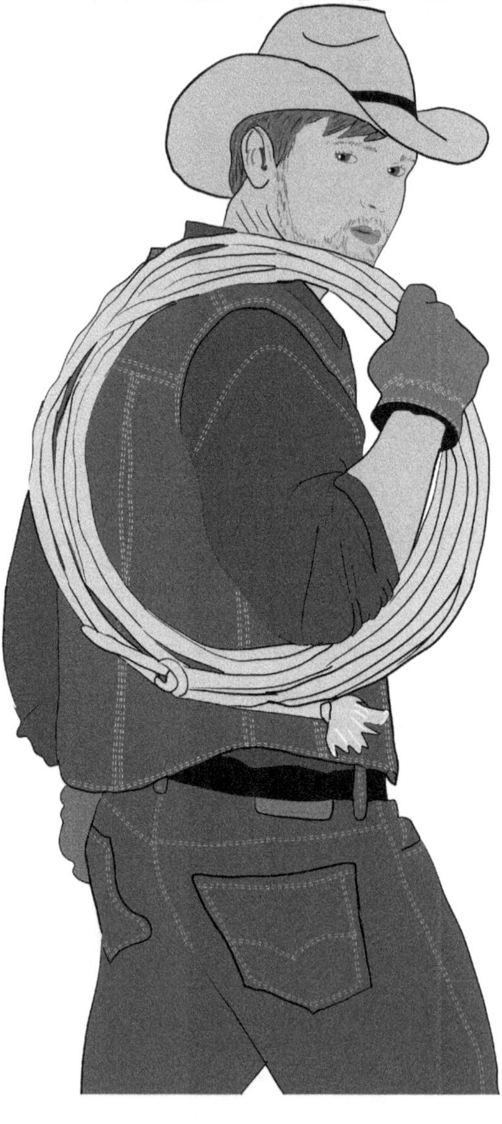

Forty-Two
42

"Lukey!" Ma came running across the kitchen. Ma only called me that when she missed me. It had been two and a half months since I left home. If I had known it would have been that long, I'm not sure I would have gone in the first place. If I knew Lucy was expecting, I know I wouldn't have left home.

"Ma." I hugged her.

"Are you okay?" She grabbed each side of my cheeks and pulled me closer to her face. She kissed each cheek.

"Yes, Ma. I'm better." I chuckled.

"I would have made pie if I knew you were coming home today!" Ma let go of my face, horrified.

"That's okay Ma. You can make all of my favorites tomorrow." I grinned.

"I will." Ma laughed.

"I hear supper is ready?" I looked over her shoulder and waved at Lucy's Pa.

"Glad to have you home." He smiled back and waved.

"I can sure say I missed being home, and I definitely missed Ma's cooking." I grinned at mother.

"Sit down, so we can pray and eat." My Ma blushed.

"Yes, Ma'am." I grinned. "Lucy." I held out a chair for her.

"Thank you." A shy smile was on my wife's face as she slid into her spot.

I sat down beside her and held out my hand for her. Lucy bit her beautiful lip and took my hand. I rested it on the table. I missed my wife's touch. A hand would have to do for now. We had a lot of time to make up for.

"Let's say grace." Lucy's father spoke up.

We all bowed our heads.

"Thank you for bringing Luke home to us safely. Thank you for the food. Thank you for the hands that prepared it. Lord, we thank you for your provision. In

Jesus' name, amen." His head came up with a smile on his lips. "We're all happy to have you home, son."

"Thank you, sir." I smiled at him and squeezed Lucy's hand. I glanced at my beautiful wife. She nodded. "Apparently, Lucy is really good at keeping secrets." I smiled at her. "We're going to have a baby."

"What?" Beth Ann's mouth fell open. "Why didn't you say something?"

Lucy laughed. "I didn't even tell Luke. He guessed."

"Congratulations." Lucy's Pa smiled proudly.

"You should have said something." Ma hurried over to hug us both.

Lucy smiled and shrugged slightly. She never looked more beautiful than she did right now. I was going to be a Pa. We were a real family now; me, Lucy, and the baby.

Having a baby meant one more mouth to feed. I mulled over the thought, and decided that I was okay with that. My thoughts drifted to our home; we might be adding to the house sooner than I thought.

Laughter bubbled around the table as the food was passed between each family member. I filled up my plate. The first bite melted in my mouth. No one cooked like Ma.

"How is the leg feeling?" I pointed my fork at my father-in-law.

"I feel when the rain is coming now." He chuckled.

"Pa walks real good now." Beth Ann spoke up.

"That's good to hear." I nodded my head and took another bite of my food.

"It's good to have you home." Ma smiled at me.

"It's good to be home." I squeezed Lucy's hand under the table.

Lucy smiled at me, and my heart bubbled with love. I missed her so much while I was at Uncle Billy's house. My aunt and uncle were good to me while I was there, but Lucy was my home now. It wouldn't hurt my feelings if I never left the farm again.

Lucy

Forty-Three
43

I was happy Luke was home. I crawled closer to Luke and put my arms around him. I felt his lips on my temple.

"Did I mention that you're not allowed to leave again?" I whispered.

Luke chuckled. "I hear you, Sweetheart."

"Good." I didn't want to let him go.

"So what should we name our son? Luke Jr.?" Luke whispered into my ear.

"And if it is a girl?" I challenged.

"Lucy Jr." He whispered.

I giggled. "Won't that be confusing?"

"Two Lukes? Or two Lucys?" Luke's tone was teasing.

"Both." I laughed.

"So, that's a no?" My husband chuckled.

"Right." I giggled.

"So, it's a yes?" My husband teased.

"No!" I laughed again.

"Then what is it?" Luke was grinning from ear to ear.

"We need to pick something else." I giggled again.

This is the happiest that I've been in months. Luke brought out a side of me that I hardly recognized. He was different with me too.

"We have time." Luke pulled me closer.

"We do." I nodded my head.

"If you can't tell, I'm happy to be a Pa." Luke whispered in my ear.

"I'm real glad. I think you'll be a good father." I smiled.

"I think you'll make a real good Ma too." Luke rubbed my arm.

"I hope so. I don't know much about raising children." I swallowed.

I knew I wouldn't be like other mothers. I wasn't the kind of woman that like to stay in the kitchen or do dishes. I like to work with my hands. My favorite place was with Luke or the barn. The only thing I knew how to do right was take care of animals and run this place. I hope it would be enough for Luke and the baby.

"I don't want to hear you talk like that. You are perfect just the way you are." Luke turned to face me.

I remained quiet, because I wasn't sure if I agreed. I was glad that Luke felt that way. He had a way of letting me be myself.

"You helped raise Beth Ann, didn't you?" Luke tried another angle.

I nodded my head.

"She seems to be turning out all right." Luke brushed the hair out of my face.

"Yeah, I think so. She still has some growing to do." I smiled.

"That's okay, because you still have some teaching to do, right?" My husband smiled at me.

"I reckon you're right." I stared into Luke's face. "I really missed you."

"I think I missed you more." Luke's warm breath hit my face.

We shared a long, slow kiss.

"I love you with all my heart, Sweetheart."

"I love you, Luke." I kissed him again.

"Kissing you is one of the things I missed the most." Luke grinned.

I giggled.

"Do you know how beautiful you are?" My husband whispered.

"Being beautiful isn't something I've ever been accused of." I shook my head.

"You are the most beautiful woman I've ever seen." Luke kissed my neck and made me giggle.

"Okay, I'll believe you." I giggled again.

"I love you." Luke put his hand on my stomach.

I couldn't wait to meet our son or daughter. I put my hand on my stomach beside my husband's hand. I wondered if our baby could hear Luke's voice. I hoped so. He had a nice voice.

"Do you think our baby can hear us?" I bit my lower lip.

"Good question." Luke's eyes met mine.

"I think you should sing to him or her." I giggled.

"Is that your way of saying you missed my singing voice?" Luke chuckled.

"Maybe a little?" I held up my thumb and index finger.

"Okay, let me think for a minute." Luke stared at the ceiling. "Okay, I got one."

Luke

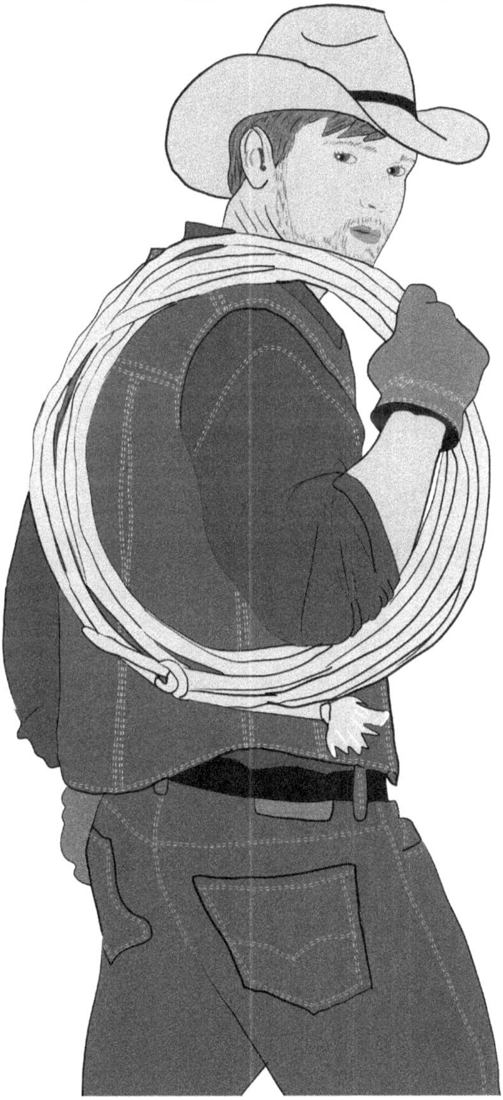

Forty-Four
44

"Lucy, that's too heavy for you!" I ran over and took the bag out of Lucy's hands. "Where do you want it?"

Lucy pointed.

I put the bag down. "Lucy, that's too heavy for you right now while you are with child."

"I'm not broken." Lucy put her hand on her hip.

"I know, and I want to keep it that way." I leaned closer.

Lucy let out a deep breath. "You're overreacting." She turned and walked away from me.

"What are you talking about?" I stomped after her.

"Nothing." Lucy muttered.

"Is this one of those women things?" I caught her hand and held her in place.

"It's just since you came back... well.." Lucy pulled her hand out of mine. "Never mind."

"Sweetheart, what's wrong?" I leaned over her.

"It's just that ever since you found out I was expecting that ... that..." My wife avoided my gaze.

"That, what?" I touched her shoulder.

"You don't let me do anything anymore!" Lucy yelled at me.

I took a step back. Lucy almost never yelled. I messed up, and I wasn't sure how. Is this where I say I'm sorry? I don't know.

"I was trying to help." I bit my lower lip once and shook my head.

"I know." Lucy took my hand. "But I can't sit around for 6 months and do nothing." Her voice was off. I'm pretty sure she was mad.

"You can if you want to." I took off my hat and readjusted my hair with my hand before putting my hat back on.

"No Luke, I can't." The temper in those pretty blue eyes flared. I was in trouble.

"What do you want from me, Sweetheart?" I put my hands out, feeling helpless. I could milk a cow, plow up the land, and build a house, but I didn't know how to fix this.

"I want you to stop treating me like I am something breakable." Lucy's nose flared.

I had seen my horse make that face when she was about to run away from me. I had to do something to fix this quick.

God, you're going to have to help me with this woman. I prayed.

"Sweetheart, I'm sorry... for... what I did." I scratched my head.

"Do you know what you did?" Lucy put her hand on her hip again.

"Not really, but Pa always told me that if I didn't know why a woman was mad, I should say I was sorry." I clenched my teeth together and tried to fake a smile.

Lucy's lip twitched, and then she laughed. "Your Pa was a smart man."

I nodded my head. It was probably best to stay quiet. Talking too much made women mad sometimes.

"Just so you know, I'm going to work until this baby is born." Lucy poked my chest.

I nodded.

"Ask me if I want help; don't do it for me unless I ask." Lucy's voice was firm.

"That's fair." I nodded again. "Will you leave the heavy lifting to me?"

"I guess so." My wife grumbled.

"Thank you." I couldn't help smiling.

"What's that look for?" She put her hand on my chest.

"I'm glad you're mine. Does this mean I am forgiven?" I grinned.

Lucy's eyes searched mine and finally nodded. She stepped closer and put her hand on my chest. "I love you Luke, but you're not going to stop me from running this farm how it needs to run."

"I'm not stopping you." I shook my head no.

Lucy's eyebrows went up.

"I want you to both be safe." I put my hand on her bulging stomach. Since I came home two weeks ago, she was starting to show.

"We are safe." She whispered.

"Let me do the heavy stuff, Sweetheart. Just until our son is here." I felt the warm embers of a fire starting to brew between us.

"Or daughter." Lucy smirked.

"Until baby Larson is here." I grinned and leaned in for a kiss.

I loved this woman with all I knew how to love. I sure didn't want to be on her bad side. When I pulled away. She was still smiling. I must have fixed it.

"It's a good thing you're handsome." Lucy rolled her eyes.

"You think I'm handsome, Lucy?" I couldn't help grinning.

Lucy laughed and pushed my chest gently. "Searching for a compliment?"

"Yes, Ma'am." I grinned.

"You're handsome, Mr. Larson." Lucy kissed me and walked away.

"Where are you going?" I rushed after her.

Lucy glanced over her shoulder and laughed without answering me. I don't know what kind of hold this woman had over me, but she had it tighter than anyone else ever had. I'd do anything in my power to protect her.

I cornered her at the end of the barn. "I love you, Sweetheart."

"I love you too." Lucy's eyes sparkled.

For the hundredth time, I sent up a prayer of thanks that I had seen her ad. I couldn't imagine another man being around my wife.

Lucy

Forty-Five
45

I groaned.

"What's wrong?" Luke came running from the other room. "Are you okay?"

"It doesn't fit!" I wanted to cry. How was I supposed to get any work done if I didn't have any clothes to wear?

A smile crept up on Luke's face.

"Don't look at me like that when I'm mad." I huffed.

"I wouldn't dream of it." He walked to the other side of the room. "Try this." He handed me one of his button up shirts.

I took it and looked up into his dark eyes. "If this fits, then I'm bigger than I think I am."

Luke chuckled. "You're perfect just the way you are." He kissed my temple.

I slid the shirt on and started buttoning it. The sleeves made me feel like I was playing dress up. I flapped my arms. Luke laughed and took the sleeve in his hand and folded it up to my elbows.

"Better?" His touch was tender and his voice was gentle. It made me feel guilty for getting so upset in the first place.

"Thank you." I nodded. "You missed one." I handed him my other arm.

Luke laughed again. "Sure thing, Sweetheart." He rolled up the other sleeve.

I pinched the stomach area and pulled it out. I had two more inches, so the baby couldn't get bigger than that or I would be stuck at home under the sheets, because I had nothing to wear.

"We can let out a few of my shirts later if we need to. I don't mind." Luke touched my cheek with the palm of my hand.

"Then we'd have to get you replacements!" My jaw fell open.

Luke laughed. "I love you, Sweetheart. I'd do anything for you, you know that. Right?"

I nodded. "I love you too."

We shared a kiss.

"Why do you have to be all sweet when I'm trying to be mad?" I huffed.

"One, you are cute." My husband smiled.

"Cute? I look like a cow. I'm huge." I wasn't sure if he was blind.

Luke chuckled.

"See! You laughed." I made my way into the main room.

"And two, you're carrying our baby." Luke stepped behind me, and wrapped his arms around me.

"Basically, I'm doing the hard part." I picked a cookie off the table Luke made and ate it.

"Basically." Luke chuckled.

"You make it really hard to leave the house when you don't let go." I glanced over my shoulder with a smile.

"Part of my charm." Luke kissed my temple and let me go. "I've got to get the wagon ready."

"Okay." I nodded my head.

I tried to put on my boots and failed. My stomach was too big. I heard the sound of the door opening. Luke came in. His gaze went to my feet. They were halfway in my boots and halfway not in my boots.

"Would you like some help?" Luke had a grin on his face.

"Yes." I had a few tears escape.

"Oh, Sweetheart." Luke crossed the room. "I didn't mean to laugh."

I cried against his shirt. Luke rubbed my back, which made me feel worse. I've never been this emotional in my life. I used to think I was a reasonable person until I carried this baby. All of that went straight out the window.

"I'm sorry, Luke." I let out a deep breath.

"It's okay." My husband kissed my temple and helped me with my boots.

"It's not okay." I sobbed.

"Whoa." Luke wrapped his arms around me. "There. There." He rubbed my back.

"That's how you talk when you train Jethro." I sobbed.

Jethro was our most skittish horse. Luke had a way of calming him down when no one else could. I felt Luke's chest vibrate as he laughed.

"You're laughing." I sobbed.

"I'm laughing WITH you." Luke whispered.

"But I'm not laughing." I continued sobbing.

"I'm sorry, Sweetheart." Luke kissed the top of my head.

"Thank you for helping with my boots." I made a sad face.

"Are you ready to head out?" Luke tucked my hair behind my ear.

I nodded my head.

"I love you." Luke kissed my hand and led me out of the house.

"Thank you, Luke." I pouted.

Luke helped me get into the wagon. He climbed up on the other side of the wagon and flipped the reins. We passed the planted fields. They were the most beautiful sight in the world. My husband had been picking up my slack on the farm ever since he found out I was with child.

"You and Tommy did a great job getting these fields ready. I don't remember the last time these fields have been worked, if I'm honest." I smiled at my husband.

"I'm glad we were able to get everything done in time. Lord willing, if the weather cooperates, it should be a good crop." My husband flashed me a smile.

"I love you; do you know that?" I moved closer.

Luke wrapped his arm around me. "I'm glad. I love you too."

Luke

Forty-Six
46

This pregnancy was going to kill me. I loved Lucy with all of my heart, but I wasn't sure what to do about the mood swings. First she was normal, then she was angry, and then she was crying. Most of the time, she still wanted me to kiss her, so I focused on that.

"I'm hungry." Lucy complained as she walked out of the bedroom.

"I know, Sweetheart." I cracked opened the egg and put it in the iron skillet. She woke me up twenty minutes ago complaining that she needed scrambled eggs and she needed them now. I had gone as fast as possible, but it took a few minutes to put on clothes, build the fire, and get the eggs from the chicken coop in the dark. They were so confused when I came in. I can't say I blame them; this was not my normal sleep schedule either. I was up cooking because I didn't want a crying woman on my hands again.

Lucy walked over behind me and held me. I could feel our baby between us. Our baby. This was the woman I loved. I used the spatula on the eggs.

"Thank you." Lucy laid her head against my back.

"Anytime Sweetheart." I prepared the eggs. "Get me a plate."

Lucy walked over to the dishes and handed me a plate. I put the eggs on the plate and moved the pan out of the way. It would be a while before the fire died down. Lucy got herself a fork and sat down with the plate.

"This is perfect." She moaned when she took a bite.

"I'm glad you like it." I put the coffee water on top of the fire and sat down at the kitchen table with my wife.

Lucy held out her hand to me, and I took it. I smiled at my wife. It was all worth it if she was happy.

"Oh, no." Lucy held her mouth and ran outside.

I stood up and ran after Lucy. I wasn't sure what was wrong. She made it to the edge of the treeline before she vomited all over the ground. I made a face.

"Don't come this way." Lucy tried to wave me off.

"Sickness and health, Sweetheart." I made my way over to my wife.

I wasn't sure what kind of mood swing I was about to get. Lucy bent over and vomited again. I stayed where I was and waited for her to be done.

"I think I'm done." Lucy gave me a sad smile.

"I'm sorry, Sweetheart." I opened my arms, and she walked into them.

"I don't think I can have eggs anymore. They sounded so good, and now they sound gross." Lucy sounded pitiful.

"Okay, no more eggs." I rubbed her back.

"I made it really far from the house." Lucy smiled at me proudly.

"Yes, you did." I chuckled.

"I'm really going to miss eggs." Lucy pouted.

"I know." I kissed her forehead.

"Let's head to the main house." Lucy walked away from me.

"I thought you decided to stay home today." I called after her.

"I changed my mind. I want to pick up the baby quilt Millie is making." Lucy was already halfway to the barn.

I closed my eyes and let out a deep breath. I couldn't wait to have my wife back. I headed into the house and put out the fire and tossed the eggs outside by the treeline.

"Are you coming?" Lucy already had the wagon out of the barn and was ready to go.

"Yes, I'm coming." I put the iron skillet into the house and climbed up on the wagon beside my wife.

Lucy

Forty-Seven
47

The sun was just peeking up over the horizon. When Luke and I pulled up to the barn. I can't believe eggs made me feel like that! What kind of country girl was I?

"Would you like some help?" Luke offered his hands to me.

"I better." I had an easier time getting into the wagon than I did getting out of it.

"Morning, Tommy." I greeted my brother-in-law.

"Morning, Lucy." Tommy was already milking one of the cows.

"Did you feed the animals?" Luke walked over to his brother.

"Sure did, first thing. Do you want to milk a cow?" Tommy pointed to the cow in its stall.

"Shore." Luke let out the cow and pulled up a stool.

"I'll go ask your Ma about that quilt." I started walking to the main house, and decided I had to pee.

I changed directions and made a beeline for the outhouse. I stood up after peeing and had to pee again, so I sat back down. I sat there for a minute and then tried again and I had to pee again.

Knock. Knock. Knock.

"Someone's in here!" I called through the locked door.

"Lucy, it's Luke. Is everything okay in there?" My husband's patience made me feel even more guilty.

"I can't stop." I was on the verge of tears.

"Can't stop what, Sweetheart?" Luke's deep voice was concerned.

"Every time I stand up, I pee." I complained.

Luke started chuckling.

"It's not funny!" I pouted.

"Course, it's not." Luke laughed again.

"Luke!" I stood up and this time pee didn't come out.

I unlocked the outhouse and walked out. Luke was trying not to smile. I slammed the outhouse door behind me and marched to the main house.

Luke sauntered in front of me and opened the door. Millie was pulling fresh rolls out of the oven. Beth Ann was pouring coffee.

"Good morning, Lucy." My sister grinned.

I sat down. I was huge. I didn't want to go any-where. Why did I come here?

"Are you hungry?" Millie put the plate of rolls on the table.

I nodded my head.

"Let me get the eggs going." Millie turned around.

"NO EGGS." Luke's voice bellowed.

"Why on Earth not?" Pa sat down.

"Trust me, it's not a good idea." Luke glanced at me.

Millie's gaze landed on me. She gave me an un-derstanding smile and nodded. My stomach growled.

"Was that you?" Beth Ann's eyes were wide.

"It was the baby." I pointed at my stomach and everyone laughed.

After everyone ate, I sat at the table and waited for Beth Ann to clean up. I know I should be helping out, but I wasn't up for moving at all. Luke had gone outside with Pa and Tommy. I was glad Pa was doing better, because I wasn't much help these days.

"Here is the quilt." Millie handed me a pile.

On top was the cutest little gown. I held it up and started crying. It was perfect.

"Lucy, are you okay?" Beth Ann stopped moving.

"I'm fine." Tears fell down my cheeks.

"Of course you are." Millie held me.

My sister was more concerned than ever. I picked up each little outfit and refolded it. I needed to go set up the baby's room, Luke added on earlier this summer. I stood up and kissed Millie's cheek.

"It's all perfect. Thank you." I picked up the items and walked out the door.

"Beth Ann, get a basket of bread ready for Lucy and Luke." Millie ordered.

"Yes, Ma'am." Beth Ann started filling a basket with bread.

I walked out of the house and made my way to the barn. Luke, Pa, and Tommy were jawing. A waste of a perfectly good day.

"I'm ready to go." I told my husband.

"Shore." Luke was startled, but he got the wagon ready to go anyway.

"Here you go, Lucy." Beth Ann ran up and put a basket in the back of the wagon. "I put your favorite cookies in there too."

"Thank you." I smiled at my sister.

"Do you need help?" Pa asked.

"Might be best." I hated asking for help.

"No trouble." Pa helped me get into the wagon.

"Ready?" Luke hopped up into the wagon.

I nodded my head.

"Take care now." Pa tapped the side of the wagon as we took off.

I waved to my Pa, and we were on our way back home.

"Are you feeling okay?" Luke asked me once we were out of earshot.

"I feel fine. We have a lot to do today and it ain't going to happen sitting around jawing." I fingered the baby clothes in my lap.

"Alright." Luke chuckled. "What do you have in mind?"

"First off, I want you to finish up that crib today and put it in the baby's room. I'm going to put a quilt in it, and then use the one your Ma made to make the bed look nice." I pointed to the baby quilt in my lap.

"That's real nice." Luke nodded his approval.

"Your Ma did a good job." I agreed.

"Anything else?" Luke hedged.

"I was wanting to move our bed to the other wall, so we can hear the baby at night." I mulled over what else needed to be done.

"Shore." Luke led the horses to the house and helped me down.

"Thank you." I smiled shyly.

"I'll take care of the horses and head in." Luke kissed my temple.

I walked inside of the house. It seemed too daunting. I let out a deep breath and decided I needed a nap.

I put the baby items on the trunk and laid down and fell asleep.

I felt something on my forehead. I tried to push it away. I heard my husband's warm chuckle.

"Luke, what time is it?" I yawned.

"You slept past meal time. I put the crib in the bedroom like you asked." Luke smiled.

I touched his cheek. He was the gentlest, strongest man I knew. I smiled at him with love.

"Thank you, you're really nice." I yawned and got up.

"I think you're really nice too." Luke chuckled.

"Ut oh." I winced.

"What's wrong?" Luke was immediately concerned.

"I think I peed my pants, but only a little." I stuck out my bottom lip.

Luke busted out laughing.

"It's not funny!" I stood to my feet.

"It was only a little." My husband stood up, giggling.

I stood up and shuffled my way out to the out-house. I managed to sit down in the outhouse before it became a serious issue. My legs went numb, because I sat in the outhouse for so long.

"Are you okay in there?" Luke called through the door.

"I'm fine." I frowned.

"I brought pants for you." Luke opened the door and handed me the pants.

"Thanks." I took them.

Luke closed the door and waited. I FINALLY made my way out of the outhouse. The sun told me that it was about midday. That meant I still had time to put everything together.

"I want to see the baby's room." I carried the pants toward the house and dropped them just inside the door. I had a lot of work to do and not a lot of time to do it.

Luke

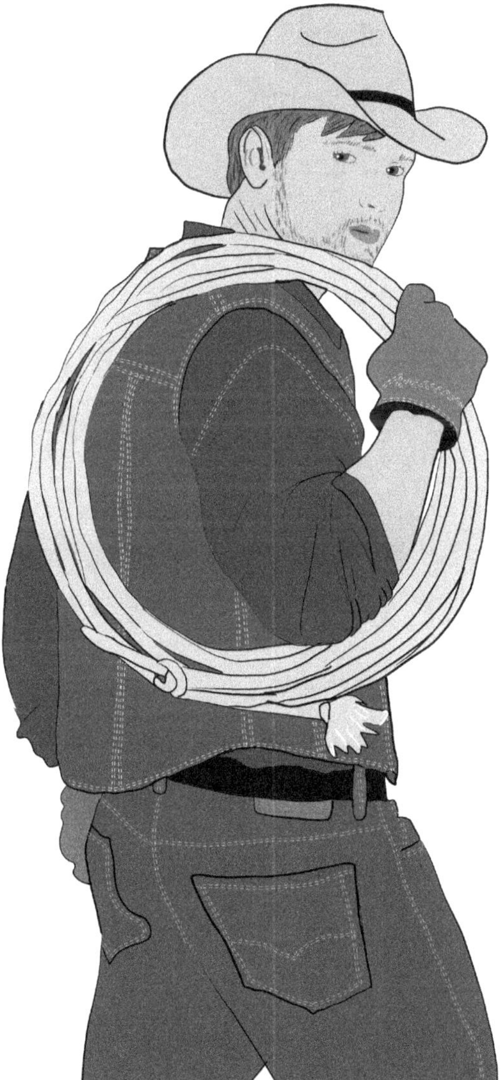

Forty-Eight
48

I moved my son closer to me. Everything we went through the last 9 months made it worth it. He was perfect. Lucy was safe.

In this moment, I knew that my life would never be the same again. It was a heavy responsibility, but life with my son and Lucy was better than I could imagine.

"Isn't he perfect?" Lucy put a hand on his little cheek.

"Yes, he is. Just like his mother." I winked at my wife.

Lucy rolled her eyes.

"What?" I reached for her hand.

"I have a baby and you are right back to trying to sweet-talk me." Lucy laced her fingers through mine.

"I go with what works." I chuckled.

"I was thinking, that maybe we should name him after your Pa." Lucy's beautiful blue eyes searched mine.

"Really?" I was stunned.

"Do you think that's a good idea?" Lucy waited for my answer.

"That means a lot, Sweetheart." I wasn't really a crier, but I had to blink a few times to keep back the tears.

The only thing that would make this moment any better was if my Pa was here to meet my son. I knew that it wasn't possible, but he would have been the best grandpa. I missed him every day.

"Do you think it's too soon for him to travel?" Lucy frowned.

"Babies ride in wagons all the time. You just had a baby. Are you able to travel?" I wanted Lucy to be safe.

"I want to show Beth Ann and Pa." Lucy grinned.

"Okay." I leaned forward and placed a kiss on my wife's lips.

A fire burned between us. I'd never loved anyone more than my wife and son. I placed a gentle kiss on my son's head and handed him to Lucy.

"I'll try to get him to eat before we go." Lucy caressed his little head with love.

"Okay. I'll be back in a minute." I kissed my wife quickly on the lips and then kissed my son on his forehead.

I whistled all the way out to the barn.

"Guess what?" I whispered to my horse.

My horse neighed.

"I'm a Pa." I patted his side.

My horse shook his head.

"Really, I am. You're going to meet him in a little bit." I patted him.

It didn't take me long to get the wagon ready and pull it in front of our home. Our son came right before harvest time. It was hard to believe that a year ago that I didn't even know Lucy.

I walked in and waited until our son had finished eating. Lucy handed him to me and we made our way to the wagon. I was with my FAMILY. My heart was full of pride. This love that I felt was stronger than I could ever have imagined.

"This is so much easier without him sitting on me." Lucy put her hand on her stomach where he used to be.

"I bet it is." I handed him over, and the three of us made our way to the main house.

"Luke! Where have you been? Ma was going to send me to get you if you didn't show up today." Tommy met us at the wagon. "What's that?" He pointed to the bundle in Lucy's arms.

"That is Gabe Larson." I smiled.

"Like Pa?" Tommy's mouth opened.

"Shore is." I hopped down and walked to the other side of the wagon.

Lucy handed me Gabe, and Tommy stepped up to help her down. Lucy's eyebrows went up as he helped, but she didn't say anything. I swayed back and forth. I didn't know a whole lot about babies, but I think they liked that.

"Ma! Ma! Come quick!" Tommy went running off.

Gabe started to cry. I was going to throttle my brother when he came back. He was going to have to learn not to run around hooping and hollering.

"I'll take him." Lucy held out her hands for our son.

As soon as Gabe heard Lucy's voice, his eyes searched for her.

"I'm right here." Lucy smiled. "Everything is alright."

"I think he loves you more than he loves me. Although, I can't say I blame him. You are prettier to look at." I grinned.

Lucy laughed.

"Tommy says..." Ma came out of the house, wiping her hands on her apron.

"Do you want to meet your grandson?" Lucy smiled.

"You should have come and got me." Ma held out her hands. "I would have come." She cooed over our baby.

"Tommy, if you yell like that around my son, I'm going to deck you." I growled at my brother.

"Oh, no you won't." Ma cooed as she walked into the house.

I put two fingers to my eyes in a 'V' and back at Tommy and mouthed, yes, I will.

"Sorry, Luke." Tommy winced.

I nodded.

Ma sat down at the table. Lucy and I followed her inside the house. I pulled out the chair and Lucy sat down.

"Is that...?" Beth Ann rushed over. "Aw, you are so cute. I am Auntie Beth Ann."

I smiled. It looked like little Gabe had a lifetime of love coming up. Hopefully, a few years down the road, he would have a little brother or sister. I wanted a full house.

"We named him Gabe Larson after Luke's Pa." Lucy reached for my hand.

I met her halfway and gave her a slight squeeze. This was one of those moments that I would remember for the rest of my life. I put Lucy's hand to my lips and kissed it.

"Your Pa would have been so proud." Ma smiled at me through happy tears.

"Nice to meet you, Gabe." Beth Ann cooed. "I love you already."

Lucy's Pa walked in. He leaned over Ma's shoulder and smiled at our son, before walking over and rubbing my shoulders and patting me on the back. I knew he cared about me, Tommy, and Ma.

This family was plum full of love, and I knew that meeting Lucy was the best thing I could have done for me. She gave me the room to be the man I wanted to be, and she supported my dreams. I couldn't ask for more out of my wife than that.

8 Years Later...

Lucy

Forty-Nine
EPILOGUE

"Hello, Ida." I cooed at my youngest daughter. "I love you."

Ida reached for my finger. I smiled. She would be walking any day now. I couldn't wait until I could get her up on a horse and teach her how to ride like had taught her brother and sister. Gabe was already well on his way to knowing everything there was to know about horses and farm life.

"Ma, Gabe won't help me pick flowers!" My daughter, Rebecca, ran up to me.

"I don't want to pick flowers!" Gabe tried to beat his sister to me.

"Sweetheart, he doesn't have to help you pick flowers." I rubbed her back.

"But then the vase will be empty." Rebecca pouted.

Rebecca put her tin cup on the table earlier this morning and declared she was going to fill it with flowers when we got back from the main house.

"Will not!" Gabe shook his head.

"What's going on here?" Luke walked up to us and folded his arms.

"Nothing, sir." Gabe shook his head.

"I need more flowers." Rebecca held up three lifeless dandelions.

"Why didn't you say so?" Luke held out his hand. "Did you know your Ma likes when I pick her flowers?" My husband winked at me.

"She does?" Rebecca walked with Luke to the larger patch of dandelions.

"I'll help you, Pa!" Gabe ran after both of them.

I shook my head. Some days, Luke had more patience with our children and other days, I did. My son was determined to walk every step Luke walked. Once again, I was glad I had married a good man. If Gabe ended up just like his father, he'd turn out more than alright.

"They are so cute at that age." Millie sat down beside of me.

"They're learning." I smiled at her.

Millie and Pa got married the year after Luke and I got hitched. They've been happy ever since. Beth Ann loved Millie as much as I did, so when they first got married, it wasn't much of a change.

"Do you have anything exciting planned for your anniversary with Pa?" I readjusted my third child in my arms.

"Not yet." Millie shook her head.

"Do you want me to see if Beth Ann and Doug can come over with their kids? Maybe we could have a party after church on Sunday?" I suggested.

"That sounds real nice." Pa walked over and picked Ida up out of my hands.

I chuckled as Pa made faces at my daughter.

"I wish Tommy would find him a good woman." Millie scowled.

"He'll get around to it one of these days." Pa tucked Ida against his chest.

Ever since Tommy turned of age, she'd been blatantly hinting it was time for him to get a family of his own. My poor brother-in-law had been thinking of every excuse in the book to avoid tying the knot. I didn't blame him one bit. He was still young; he had time.

"Did I miss the party?" Tommy sauntered over.

"We were just talking about finding you a good girl to settle down with." Millie didn't bother hiding the conversation one bit.

Tommy flinched. "What was that Luke? Did you say you needed me?" He backed away from us and took off towards Luke and the kids.

I laughed. "I don't think I've ever seen Tommy move that quick."

"Me neither." Pa chuckled.

"He needs a woman." Millie's eyes flew to her son.

"If he isn't married by the time he is 22, I'll put an ad: Looking for a mail-order-bride for my brother-in-law in Fairfield County." I wrapped my arm around Millie.

"Promise?" My mother-in-law laughed.

"Shore." I grinned.

Heidi Harris

Check Out My Website,

Facebook, Instagram, TikTok, and my links to my other

series on Amazon

www.heidiharriswrites.com

https://linktr.ee/heidiharriswrites